The ENGLISH ROSE

Praise for The English Rose

"I was immediately taken back to the charm and enchantment of medieval kingdoms with Sarah Hinze's *The English Rose* in this compelling series illuminating the life and times of her ancestor, Ada de Warenne. You will rejoice with, weep, and cheer for this remarkable young woman whose fortitude and faith carried her through the uncertainty, dangers, and intrigues of the life of the Anglo-Norman nobility."

—David J. Larsen, Ph.D.

"Sarah Hinze delivers in this riveting, sumptuous tale."

—Jenni James, Award winning screenwriter
and author of over fifty books

The ENGLISH ROSE

ADA DE WARENNE MEETS
HENRY PRINCE OF SCOTS

BOOK ONE OF
THE PAWN SERIES

SARAH HINZE

Three Orchard
Productions

Also by Sarah Hinze

Nonfiction

Memories of Heaven
The Announcing Dream
The Castaways: New Evidence Supporting the Rights of the Unborn Child
Songs of the Morning Stars
Coming from the Light
The Memory Catcher: Memoirs of Sarah Hinze
Remembering Heaven (the book) Coming 2024

Historical Fiction

The English Rose: Ada de Warenne Meets Henry Prince of Scots
Book One The Pawn Series
A Pawn for a King: Ada de Warenne, Scottish Princess
Book Two The Pawn Series

Coming in 2025
Queen Mother to the Kings of Scots, Ada de Warenne 1123-1178
Book Three The Pawn Series

Documentary Film

Remembering Heaven (2021)
Nominated at the 2021 International Christian Film Festival
Winner of Best Documentary and People's Choice Award at
the 2021 LDS Film Festival.
Winner of Best Documentary at the 2021 Utah Film Festival.
Winner of "Best of State" in Utah
https://bestofstate.org April 2021

Author's Note

While writing *A Pawn for a King* I came across the most important historical reference that is the heart of *The English Rose*.

Orderic Vitalis was an English chronicler and monk, the author of *The Ecclesiastical History of England and Normandy,* and a contemporary of Ada and Henry. His view of Henry's feelings towards Ada was that "as Henry was much attached to Adeline, daughter of William, Earl of Surrey, he demanded her in marriage." (*Historia Ecclesiastica, Vol. IV*).

So although the marriage clearly was a "pawn marriage" in which both Ada and Henry were ordered by the king to marry as part of a treaty, thus serving a political, diplomatic purpose, Ada and Henry's story was surely rare in that it included true attraction, romance, and deep, lasting love. Prince Henry was beloved by the people of Scotland and was said to be one of the most handsome men people had ever seen.

Additional historical data concerning this book, including a timeline is on my website at www.sarahhinze/books.com

Sarah Hinze

Find all of Sarah's books and purchase at
https://sarahhinze.com/books
Amazon.com
Barnes&Noble.com
and other online retailers

Three Orchard Productions, LLC

Copyright © 2024 by Sarah Hinze
Published by Three Orchard Productions, LLC
Mesa, AZ
Printed in the United States of America

This is a work of fiction.

This story is a work of fiction. With the exception of recognized historical figures and events, all characters and events are the product of the author's imagination. Some characters and historical events have been altered for dramatic effect.

ISBN: 978-1-7334242-1-9

Cover design by
Adrienne Quintana
Pink Umbrella Books

BISAC Subject Headings

FIC014000   FICTION / Historical / General

HIS037010   HISTORY / Europe / Medieval

FIC042030   FICTION / Christian / Historical

FIC027050   FICTION / Romance / Historical / General

FIC044000   FICTION / Women

Dedicated to

My 25th great grandmother Ada de Warenne and her beloved Henry

as well as her vast posterity.

I have been delighted to meet many of you

and hope to meet more of you along the way.

I vow to thee, my country, all earthly things above,
Entire and whole and perfect, the service of my love;

from the poem and hymn
I Vow to Thee, my Country
by Sir Cecil Spring Rice

CHAPTER ONE

Anno Domini 1136
Reigate, Surrey, England

I poked my needle into the linen, mindlessly embroidering a cowslip flower with its egg-yolk-yellow bloom. The table cover I worked on would eventually be added to the other home necessities and clothing in my *trousseau*, waiting for the day I married. For I knew the day would surely come whether I wanted it to or not. I had no say in who I would wed and expected him to be someone three times my age, widowed, bald, and with children.

Because of my nobility I'd been told all my life that duty to king and kingdom was my guide, and I must bow to its bequests. Finding a husband for the kingdom's political gain would be one of those endowments placed upon me.

The whole idea left me cold and wearisome, and I was trying to be resigned to my fate. I wished I could have the patient valor of my sister Gundred who lived to serve her king no matter the sacrifice. When she was thirteen, she'd married a man of one and fifty. And she went to the altar willingly. I sighed my lament.

My mother, *Maman*, glanced over at me, questioning my sigh with an expression of curiosity. She also sat sewing in the sun-brightened solar, a private room used only by my family, located on the floor above the Great Hall of our castle.

A servant came to the door and bowed. "Lord de Warenne requires your attendance in the Great Hall, m'lady."

Maman set aside her sewing and left to meet my father, *Père*, below.

I strained my ears in an attempt to determine if something unusual was happening downstairs. The days had been quiet and dreary, and I hoped for adventure or at least a new activity. After hearing nothing, I poked my needle into the linen, working out the next stitch.

A short time later, my maid Clare hurried into the room. "We must dress you in your finest tunic."

"Whyever for?" I followed her out of the solar to my bedchamber.

"Your *maman* asked me to hold my tongue, but you will want to look your best." She replied in French as she brought from the wardrobe my favorite golden wheat-colored tunic, sewn with pearls on the bodice and a jeweled leather belt. She laid it on the bed and helped me undress.

"Who is here?" I was the youngest in the family and hated being treated like an infant who couldn't know what the adults did.

Clare scowled but I could tell she enjoyed having a secret. She was sixteen, two years older than me, but she often pretended she was as old as my mother and could command me. In a nice way. She was a servant after all. A sly smile slipped but she quickly covered it with her hand. "Stop asking. I'll not bring the ire of my mistress." With haste she washed and dressed me.

I sat for her to style my hair. I'd not given my appearance a thought since my morning's ride on my horse Cooper.

Clare unbraided my hair, letting it fall to my waist, brushed it to a shine, then re-braided it with ivory silk ribbons, a strong contrast to my red hair. "Quickly now." She pulled me out the door and gave a budge toward the stairs. "You mustn't keep your guests waiting."

Before descending, I paused a moment and took a calming breath. Who would come to Reigate unannounced? Someone of great importance it seemed.

The aroma of roasted duck greeted me as I entered the Great Hall. The servants busily carried trays laden with fruits and meats, placing them in the center of the table for what looked like a grand feast.

And then I saw him from the side—handsomer than last we met, with broader shoulders—sitting on a cushioned chair with an outstretched leg bound in splints resting on a hassock.

My breath caught and I quickly retreated a few steps into the entry gallery where he couldn't see me. Between two paintings of illustrious ancestors, I pressed myself against the cool stones of the castle wall and brought my hands to my warm cheeks, which had heated with the memory of when I'd met him last. I prayed he'd forgotten the episode. It had been three years ago, when I was only eleven, and my half-brother Robert had arrived for a visit. My parents had planned a feast to honor Robert's stay. The anticipation of the event brought an air of excitement to the castle. My spirits were lifted too, knowing my beloved sister Gundred would be among the invited guests. She'd married the year before and had moved away. I'd missed her desperately.

Autumn had crept upon us ever so silently that year, changing nature's colors as definitely and dramatically as Gundred's marriage had changed my life. The day of the feast had arrived with cold and rainy weather. Gundred arrived with her husband Geoffrey in the early afternoon.

I ran out to meet her as she dismounted her cart. "Gundy! You have come! You have come!" I fell into her embrace, noticing her protruding stomach. "Oh, *chère sœur*. I have missed you terribly!"

Nodding a greeting toward Gundred's grey-bearded husband, I then ignored him and grasped Gundy's hand, pulling her toward the wet gardens. "Let us walk together to the willow and see if the swans have flown for the winter."

Gundred resisted, placing a hand on her abdomen. "Ada, I cannot go with you now." She looked back at Geoffrey and smiled as he reached for her hand. "I must go with my husband. *Maman* will surely want to settle us into our chamber." She gazed at me with kindness, but there was something different in her eyes too.

None of the earnest and intense interest she had previously shown remained. Instead, I found an unfathomable sea of distance.

Reluctantly, I released her hand and watched her walk away, arm-in-arm with Geoffrey—her allegiance clearly shifted.

Heaviness rooted me in place until the company had all entered the castle and left me alone. As soon as the door banged shut, I ran to the pond—at first fighting back tears but finally filled with fury. I didn't need Gundred to enjoy the magic of Reigate's palatial grounds. The swans would always be loyal to me, after all.

But the pond was no comfort, as bleak and grey as the sky above it. And to my disappointment, my beloved swans had departed for warmer climes without notifying me. Gentle rain disturbed the pond's surface. Then the drops gave way, and the skies opened. A torrent poured down in earnest.

"Why, why, why!" I shrieked, hurling a stone into the murky water.

"Hoy there!" A masculine voice called.

I froze.

The rider standing next to his steed on the far side of the pond had entirely escaped my notice.

I cowered behind a dense colony of cattails and lilyturf, a flood of embarrassment washing over me. Whoever the stranger was, he had witnessed my tantrum, and was heading my direction.

The rain stopped as suddenly as it had begun. There was no possibility of retreat for me.

"Hail lass. Is all well?"

I stiffened, speechless as the young man approached, leading a great black horse behind. Handsome and tall with broad shoulders, the stranger was not yet a grown man but perhaps a knight or his squire, for a shield lay attached to the destrier's saddle.

"Are you in distress?" His words had a lilt, soft and light, as though reciting a poem. I'd heard Scot's speak before and guessed him one.

Only a few strides away now, my heart pounded erratically. I had no mind to explain my distress to this stranger from Scotland. Why could he not be gone?

I straightened and tried to pull a few of the cattails as if my whole purpose in coming had been to gather them. But the stalks were thick and hard to pull, their leaves sharp. I quickly tried some lilyturf, the short spikes of bright purple flowers came up easier. "Hail," I finally replied.

"Ah! She speaks." His eyes seemed to be laughing at me, taking in my appearance from head to toe. I must have been a ghastly sight with my wet, loose hair plastered against my face. Not to mention the mud smeared on my dress. *Maman* would be sorely disappointed.

"Are you a knight, sir?" I asked.

"Aye," He smiled. Having reached me, he tethered his horse to a nearby tree. "Though I have yet to prove myself on the field of battle." He nodded toward the pond, his brown eyes slightly mischievous. "I thought perhaps I was under attack just now."

My cheeks burned hot. "I . . . I am . . . I have . . ."

"You have an incredibly strong arm." He chuckled. "I must say that my curiosity is piqued. What did the fish do to stir your wrath?"

"My wrath had naught to do with the fish." I lifted my chin.

"Nae? Then I'm afraid you must have taken aim at me."

"Perhaps. How am I to know if you are friend or foe? You say you are a knight, but where are your colors? Are you loyal to King Henry?"

5

"You are quite a shrewd lass. I see that no enemy of the crown may safely pass on these grounds." He bowed with a grin.

I couldn't help smiling at the gesture and the compliment, even if he was being silly.

"I assure you," he said. "I am a friend. I've just come from the king's court."

I held my ground. The knight seemed kind and genuine, and he *had* come from London. I had so many questions about the goings on at court. From what I'd gathered, Gundred's marriage had been arranged there with the king's approval. "Come from King Henry's court, you say?"

"Aye." The knight smiled. His eyes appeared friendly.

"What is it like there?" Someday I would be expected to appear at court, and the king would play with my fate like an expendable pawn on his chess board. My brows scrunched together.

"'Tis quite exciting, I assure you." The knight seemed to read the look on my face. "Fine food and drink, music and dancing. I was sorry to leave."

"I should never want to go there." I pulled another lilyturf, adding it to my bouquet.

He widened his eyes. "Why ever not?"

I hesitated. The burden of my swirling thoughts had become heavy. What harm would it do to unload them on this errant knight? "Fine food and drink are no enticement to me. I know what really goes on there."

He stepped closer, mock-seriousness in his expression. "Something sinister, I fear. I can see it in your eyes. You must tell me what you know."

"Perhaps you wouldn't consider it sinister, but you might if you were in my position."

He tilted his head, the laughter gone from his eyes. "You must tell me who would wrong you at the king's court, and I vow to be your champion."

I smiled. If only this knight *could* be my champion. Imagine having someone who would challenge the king to a duel if he tried to force me to marry some old earl. I shook my head. It wasn't only the king who would decide my fate. The knight would have to do battle with my father as well. "I'm afraid there is naught you can do for me."

"My lady?"

"Never mind." I turned back toward the pond just as a red robin landed on a rock near me. I squealed involuntarily with delight. "Hail, little friend!"

"You make friends with birds?"

"Not just the birds." I reached a finger toward the robin as if I expected it to fly up and perch there. "I am a friend to all animals. But birds are a particular favorite."

"Because you bear the same markings?" He laughed.

Heat rose to my cheeks, probably bringing them nearly to the same color as my untamed red locks.

"*Non*," I replied through gritted teeth. "Because they return from the south each year and bring the summer with them."

A gust of cold wind picked up an armful of leaves, skittering them across the path. The robin flew away.

I tugged at my collar, trying to keep the cold air at bay.

The rain started again.

"Fare you well, sir." I said, turning back toward the castle. "I must go now."

"Farewell, good lass. I hope you will be kinder to those who have vexed you than you were to the fish." He smirked and gave another bow.

My face grew hot again, and I had no reply, so I ran through the rain toward home.

I soon stood before the kitchen fire to warm myself and breathed in the wonderful aroma of meat sizzling on the spit. The room bustled with last-minute preparations and the thought struck that I should have invited the knight to join our feast. If

7

my mother had been with me, she surely would have. Though my nobility almost certainly obligated me to extend hospitality to the traveler, I didn't like the way he teased. It was best that I left him standing in the rain.

"How many guests do you think are here?" I asked Cook.

He didn't look up from the food he was preparing. "At least thirty, I'd say." He glanced over as I reached for one of the tantalizing tarts with cream stacked on a silver tray. "Remove your fingers at once!" He tapped my wrist with his whisk.

I licked off the cream and started toward the door, discreetly snatching a tiny piece of gingerbread as I went by. I popped it into my mouth, savoring the sweet and spicy taste before running upstairs to change.

Guests had already begun gathering in the Great Hall when I came back down. My maid was busy filling in where needed with the arriving guests, so my hair wasn't quite dry, and I had put on by myself a soft peach-colored tunic. I'd also remembered to wash my hands and face. I hurried to stand beside *Maman* and inconspicuously scanned the room for Gundred. Would she care I was home?

William and Reginald stood by *Père*, dressed in formal attire with ermine and sable trimmings. I bit my lip. My brothers were growing older and would soon leave me too. Someday William would inherit *Père's* title and many estates, but I hoped that was far, far in the future.

The afternoon's exercise had left me famished even after eating the gingerbread. I could hear the servants gathering outside the entrance to the Great Hall with trays of fragrant food, waiting for *Maman's* order to serve.

When all the guests had arrived, she gestured them to the dining table. "*S'il vous plaît,* join us for supper." Once seated, my mother finally bid the servants to enter.

I sat across from Gundred, still angry at the way she'd snubbed me, and tried not to meet her gaze. Instead, I became mesmerized by the variety of my favorite dishes. I'd already taken several large bites before feeling someone's eyes on me from down the table. Looking up, my gaze was met by the same brown eyes I'd encountered earlier at the pond. They fixed on me with marked amusement. The knight sat to my father's right, a very distinguished seat to occupy.

The young knight's presence at our table rendered me completely unable to eat, though I still felt ravenous. Would he tell *Maman* of my unladylike behavior at the pond? She would not be pleased to hear of my angry outburst, nor of my inhospitable attitude toward the knight himself.

Sitting up taller, I attempted to look like the lady my mother was meticulously training me to become. I tried to ignore the knight's stares, but it was difficult. His eyes seemed to always catch mine when I glanced in his direction, and they were filled with unwarranted mirth.

Maman's cousin Albert and his wife were visiting from upper Normandy and sat directly across the table from the knight. Albert was a boisterous man who'd fought alongside my father in many battles. The details of their escapades were lost on me. Most had happened years ago—some before my birth—but somehow, I felt compelled to feign interest. Perhaps because I sensed my mother's mounting tension.

Already drunk, Albert drained the remainder of his goblet and wiped his mouth on his sleeve. "I'm afraid Louis and William Clito thought they had the upper hand in Brémule when they saw us on foot." He belched. "But our tight line could not be penetrated, nor flanked."

"King Henry may have his shortcomings, but his strategy on the field of battle is unmatched." *Père* raised his glass. "Long live the king!"

"Aye! Long live the king!" came the shouts from around the table. The company raised their glasses and drank.

Albert set his goblet aside and muttered, "I'm afraid no matter how long King Henry lives, he won't be able to produce an acceptable heir with Queen Matilda."

Maman's back went rigid.

"Acceptable to whom?" came a deep, clear reply from the mysterious knight, his Scottish accent stronger than I had remembered.

Albert seemed as surprised as I and turned his attention to the young man. "A worthy question indeed. And who might you be, young sir? I do not recognize your face."

The knight bowed his head. "I am Prince Henry of the Scots."

I winced. My blunder at the pond had been far more unfortunate than I had feared. *Prince Henry from Scotland!* Then his father is David, King of the Scots.

"Ah, aye!" Albert poured himself more wine. "I'm afraid many of the barons disagree with your father's support of his sister, Queen Matilda."

"My father has sworn an oath to uphold King Henry's wishes, as I presume have many of these barons of whom you speak ." Henry of Scotland finished his statement with a smile that dazzled me but seemed to have the opposite effect on Cousin Albert.

"I'm afraid their oaths may not hold. Empress Matilda's marriage to the Count of Anjou has left a bad taste in the mouth of many Normans." Albert scowled.

Maman's face blanched white.

Under the table my feet couldn't be still. My lessons about all these Matilda's had taught me *Empress* Matilda was the daughter of King Henry and his wife *Queen* Matilda. Which meant Empress Matilda was Prince Henry's first cousin.

"King Henry's alliance with Count Fulk of Anjou may yet be short lived," *Père* said. "You have, no doubt, heard that Empress Matilda is back at court?"

"Perhaps it's best to not have disagreements at the supper table," *Maman* replied, glancing uneasily at *Père*.

Though my father was loyal to King Henry, I gathered their relationship had been troubled. And from snatches of conversation I'd overheard, my father strongly disliked Empress Matilda. My mother's interjection into the conversation seemed to be begging him to hold his tongue.

"I can confirm Empress Matilda is at court," Henry of Scotland said, not picking up on *Maman's* plea. "But I assure you that the alliance with Anjou is strong. When the time comes, Empress Matilda will succeed her father, and God willing, she and Geoffrey Anjou will continue the family line."

"We shall see," Albert said. "There are those who wish otherwise."

Maman stabbed food with her knife but did not put it in her mouth.

"The count of Blois, doubtless among them," Prince Henry said, raising an eyebrow.

"Your tone would discount it." Cousin Albert leaned forward on his elbows, his face growing increasingly stern. "But Stephen Blois's claim to the throne would have merit."

The room quieted. Uncomfortable glances passed between the guests.

Were his words treason? Father always supported our king. It appeared Cousin Albert did not.

Prince Henry shook his head. "A claim that will spill much blood, I fear."

Maman cleared her throat. "There are children in the room, my dear cousin." She looked directly at Albert. "Perhaps we could change the subject to something more pleasant."

All eyes turned on me—the youngest. Even my brother Reginald stared at Albert with rounded eyes. Was he not a child also? My mouth went dry, and I wished I could sink below the table.

"Gladly, *chère*." Albert swallowed a long drink.

Stilted conversations slowly resumed among the guests.

11

Père glanced at me with a wink and half-smile.

After supper, the servants moved the table against the wall to make room for dancing. The musicians entered with dulcimer, harp, lute, and psaltery.

Relieved to escape to my favorite seat near them where I could watch undisturbed, I tapped my foot to the tunes.

The musicians swayed in unison as they strummed their instruments.

Gundred and Geoffrey had been on the other side of the table all evening, saying not a word to me. A year ago, Gundred and I would have sat together to watch the dancing. Now she stayed at Geoffrey's side, speaking quietly with my adult siblings and their spouses. If I tried to join them, I would be like a third shoe.

My half-brother, Robert de Beaumont, and his wife, Amice de Montfort, were the most handsome couple in the group. Amice wore the latest fashion from the royal court at Westminster—a purple silk kirtle belted below the waist, with sleeves that almost brushed the floor.

I continued to survey the room. Henry of Scotland seemed to have disappeared. Perhaps he was tired after a long day of riding.

Père and *Maman* danced with others within a closed circle, *Maman*'s dress flowing gracefully with each step. In the privacy of her bedchamber, she wore her hair long. In public, she wore it in braids pinned beneath her silken veiled wimple. All the married women in the room wore wimples as well, but *Maman*'s suited her especially well. I wondered if my hair would look as beautiful beneath a veil one day.

It didn't take long before I became restless. Convinced that Henry had retired for the night, I felt safe allowing myself to enjoy the merriment and stood to twirl with the music. My tunic, made of the same delicate imported silk as *Maman*'s, flowed to the floor. It swished and swayed.

The dance brought my parents near again. To my delight, *Père* swept me into his arms. "Hold on, my dear," he said and continued around the room.

Maman smiled and joined her guests.

"*Père*, how long will it be before Cooper will be ready to ride?" I asked. He'd recently given me a lovely colt.

"Soon, my love. Chadwick nearly has him trained."

I smiled broadly, slightly out of breath, as we continued to dance with guests in the circle, some singing to the tune. "Oh, I'm so pleased. I'll ride him every day!"

"I suppose I shall need to train *you* when Cooper is ready. He is not your toy, but if you treat him properly, he will be a lifelong servant and companion."

"I understand," I assured him.

The music halted, and my father bowed, beaming at me proudly.

I curtsied in return but couldn't help giggling when our eyes met.

All traces of the serious earl who had been so concerned about the succession to the English throne earlier had vanished. I loved my father more than anyone in the world.

"I'd better rescue your mother. She's warned me never to leave her in the company of the Earl of Chester when he's inebriated."

I giggled again and glanced over my shoulder as he made his way to my mother's side. He interrupted the conversation between her and the older gentleman and led her out to the dance floor.

"Your parents are a fine couple." Prince Henry's now familiar accent came from directly behind me.

I whipped around, heat rising to my cheeks and could think of no reply. I nodded awkwardly then remembered my manners and gave him a deep curtsy. "Your Royal Highness."

"You seem more content than when I met you this afternoon. May I presume you've made peace with your foe?"

"A lady should have no foes. It's unbecoming." I tried to keep my face serious as I repeated something *Maman* once told me.

Henry smirked. "A lady, certainly. I shouldn't have mentioned it."

I glanced at my parents and lowered my voice. "And I sincerely hope you'll accept my apology for failing to invite you inside."

He leaned closer and whispered, "I could not think of accepting an apology from a lady of your stature. Nor would I mention the incident to your parents for fear that they would view me in an unfavorable light. I should have introduced myself."

I couldn't contain the feeling of relief and smiled. "My parents are charitable. You need not fear that they will judge you unkindly."

"Charitable!" Henry laughed. "Am I then someone to be pitied? Poor Empress Matilda's cousin?" His demeanor changed, and the mischievous glint returned to his eyes.

I recognized that look. I'd seen it many times in my older brothers when they teased. "I know naught of Matilda, but I do worry that your words make you unpopular."

He raised his eyebrows. "Aye. I suppose a lady would rather hold her tongue than risk being unpopular."

I nodded but couldn't help blushing. "Why don't the earls like your cousin?"

"You are a curious lass with questions others would not dare to ask." Henry's smile was pleasant. "I daresay they are threatened by her. She'll take possessions and power they believe belongs to them. But if she were her poor dead brother, they would not question her right to do so. I suppose it's simply because she's a woman."

I frowned. Was it possible that an empress was just as powerless as me? "Will your father stand behind his oath?"

"My father is a man of his word." Prince Henry's face became instantly serious. He suddenly looked older than his years, which I had guessed earlier to be about eighteen.

The music stopped.

"It's getting late, and I must retire. 'Twas most gratifying to converse with you." Prince Henry bowed. "Daughter of William de Warenne, Second Earl of Surrey."

I curtsied. "You may call me Ada."

"A pleasure, Ada." He took my hand and kissed it.

"I bid you goodnight. I depart at dawn for Scone Palace. It may be some years before I return to court." He smiled and bent close. "I don't believe there is anything sinister for you to fear there. But remember my vow to be your champion, my lady."

"Hopefully, it will be a few years before I go to court. Or perhaps I'll have the good fortune to avoid it altogether."

Henry shook his head. "I'm afraid that seems unlikely. The king will insist on having such a wise and beautiful lady in his midst."

I frowned. "So he can marry me off to one of his oldest subjects," I muttered.

Henry laughed. "Ah. I can see you are wise not to be in a hurry to grow up. Enjoy being a lass for as long as you can."

My memories of when I was younger were interrupted by a servant walking by with a tray of drinks. He looked at me oddly, probably wondering why I had pushed myself up against the wall in the hallway. My face flushed with embarrassment—not at being discovered—but at once letting Prince Henry know of my fears of being wed to an older gentleman. I prayed he did not remember those words so long ago.

Taking a deep breath, I entered the Great Hall and dropped into a formal curtsy before him. Bless *Maman* for having Clare make me more presentable. "Greetings, Prince Henry," I somehow got past my lips.

He chuckled. His dark hair swept across his brow, framing brown eyes that closely inspected me. "I would stand and take your hand if I could, for I believe I am in the presence of Lady Ada de Warenne?" His face was as I had remembered it, along with that teasing, lopsided smile.

The warmth of my face must surely have been visible to him, which made me heat up all the more. Curses to the pale skin that comes with red hair. "What has happened to your leg?"

Maman swiftly entered the hall with two servants trailing behind carrying linens. "The prince was hurt in a hunting accident not far from here." She swept past me. "Ada, do your best to make him feel at home." She spoke in an unusually cold manner. Not a compassionate tone as I'd expect.

"Of course, *Maman*."

Henry must have caught her iciness because his smile dropped.

"I will make him feel welcomed," I said, more to him than to her as she moved out of the room and up the stairs. She must be preparing a room for our royal visitor. Perhaps him coming unannounced was what had put her in a mood.

Henry tried to push himself up and grimaced. "I've been told to stay put, but if you will come to me, I'll still take your hand." He held out his and smiled with a kindness I felt in my chest.

My heart fluttered, and I chided myself for the silliness of it all. I stiffly went to him and offered my hand. When his skin touched mine, my soul seemed to register the touch. I tingled from head to foot, a new and distracting feeling I both loved and hated. I loathed the way it pushed me off-balance and out of control of my body and thoughts.

He cleared his throat, a small smile tugging at the corners of his lips.

I realized I'd held his hand longer than appropriate and I quickly pulled away. "How may I make you more comfortable? Are you in pain?"

"I'm as comfortable as to be expected for a broken leg."

"Broken?" I had no idea of the seriousness of his injury. He'd been smiling and passing casual conversation! "We must get you a barber to set the bone."

"'Twas done before they brought me here. There is naught more to do but stay off it and wait the weeks it takes to heal."

Weeks? He would not be here that long, surely. "May I ask how it happened?"

"My horse threw me when a branch near us broke in the wind."

"Oh dear! How did the horse fare?"

Prince Henry laughed deeply from his chest.

I liked the sound very much.

A servant readying the table looked at him and swiftly away. She hid her smile as she left the room. It appeared I wasn't the only one attracted to this man.

"Do you worry more for the horse?" he asked.

I curtsied again, concerned I had shown disrespect. "Forgive me, of course not, but I see you here in a chair, cheerful and able to logically converse."

"Aw." A light came into his eyes. "I remember now. The robin—you are a lover of animals."

It had been several years since I'd seen Prince Henry, yet he remembered such a trivial thing. Had he thought of me as I had of him?

Remembering again how it had felt when he'd touched my hand a moment ago, I blushed.

"You need not be embarrassed about loving animals. 'Tis a commendable trait." His eyes showed such friendliness that I wished I could bring him into the solar to get to know him better. I pictured us comfortable in each other's company.

"I think I'm going to get well quickly with your kind companionship. The bonesetter said I won't be better until autumn."

So, he was going to stay for weeks. I opened my mouth. And no words came out. To my relief, the garden door opened, and *Père* strolled into the hall accompanied by another man and my brothers William and Reginald.

The stranger and *Père* were still in conversation as they walked to us. *Père* saw me and came to my side. "Ada, we are pleased to have His Majesty, King David of the Scots, and his Royal Highness,

17

Henry Mac David, Prince of Strathclyde with us. Prince Henry will be staying, but the king will return to Northumberland tomorrow. Sire, may I present my youngest daughter, Lady Ada."

I sucked in a quick breath and curtsied deeply, rising slowly. "Your Majesty." We'd never had a king visit Reigate.

A large man with a full face and ruddy complexion, the king had a kind but curious disposition that closely examined me. His full head of white hair looked as if thorough brushing wouldn't tame it. He wore hunting clothes, not the fine silks of golds, reds, and purples that our king wore. Was this common attire for a king of the Scots? I'd only ever seen Henry in the garments of a knight.

"Lady Ada, I'm sorry to burden you with the care of my son. I fear it cannot be helped, and your father tells me I leave him in capable hands." A sadness resided in the depths of his brown eyes, and I wonder what put it there. I suspected it wasn't Henry breaking his leg.

"I am delighted to serve," I said sincerely. I had been longing for a new adventure. This one just might play more on my mental state than I had anticipated.

Père gave me a side hug. "She has the compassion of her mother."

That was hardly true, but I appreciated my father complimenting me in front of these eminent people.

CHAPTER TWO

Two days after the king left, I found the prince sitting alone on the back terrace looking out over the gardens. I felt sorry for the man capable of doing naught but sitting with his leg propped up while carrying on superficial conversations with my parents. Sometimes my brothers entertained him, which he appeared to like much better. But the boys spent most of their days in the courtyard, training to be knights.

For some reason, around Prince Henry, *Maman* remained aloof.

It turned out his presence jumbled my thoughts and tightened my stomach until I felt ill. I found excuses to not be with him other than at meals and evening entertainment. But this morning, *Père* had that impatient, please-be-obedient demand in his expression when he asked me to entertain Prince Henry while he was out.

"How do you fare this day, my lord?" I asked as I stepped in front of him. "Cook has made a fresh batch of honey sweetmeats." I held out a small silver tray with the amber treats.

Prince Henry took one. "Obliged." He slipped it in his mouth. "Mmm. They remind me of my mother." He motioned to the chair beside him.

I took a seat. King David was widowed, but I knew no details. I hesitated to ask in case Prince Henry's loss was still tenderly felt. "Honey sweetmeat is my favorite," I said instead.

"Mine too."

Oh dear, I hadn't meant to bring us to common ground. Every time I felt close to Prince Henry, I fell a little more off-kilter.

"How many siblings do you have?" I asked to start conversation.

"Two. Clarice and Hodierne."

Sisters. "Are you close in age?"

"Clarice and I are but one year apart. We were quite good playmates growing up. Hodierne is five years younger."

The thought of Henry playing as a young boy brought me great delight. Of course, it made sense that he had lived a life I hadn't been part of. Over the years since we'd first met, except for the occasional, obscure thought about him at King Henry's court training for battle, I hadn't tried to imagine what that life had been like.

"And are you still close? Does Clarice still live . . .?" I realized that I could not even remember the name of the place Henry called home. "In Scotland?"

Henry sighed deeply and stared off into the distance. "Aye. I imagine she is at this very moment enjoying her daily ride through the woods that surround Scone Palace. I long for the day when I can return." He colored a little. Did he think he'd been rude by longing to be away from Reigate? He smiled sheepishly. "But I shall be happy here with this excellent taste of home. I've felt quite abandoned since my father's departure."

I had been a terrible hostess. Self-loathing creeped in with the guilt. I popped another piece of sweetmeat in my mouth, keeping it busy so I didn't need to converse until it melted away and I could think of the best thing to say. Finally, I asked, "Do you play chess?"

"Absolutely. Let's ask a servant to bring us the board."

We played for hours until I forgot myself and relaxed. I'd never liked chess but playing with Henry changed that. I enjoyed his company and the amusing stories he told about the king's court. I guessed he was trying to reduce my anxiety about going there myself, for he often reminded me that he'd be my champion, as he'd promised years before.

That evening, I sat waiting for Clare in my bedchamber with a white-bone comb in hand, thinking back on the day. I chided myself for feeling interested in Henry because I had no say in who I courted or married. I dared not develop a relationship for I surely would be hurt in the end. I decided to make him a friend instead and not worry over the future.

Maman opened the door and entered my room.

"Where is Clare?" I asked. My maid usually combed my hair.

"She's not well tonight," *Maman* said in French. "I sent her to bed." She wore her greying hair in two ribboned braids that draped over her shoulders and a jeweled gold ornament on her forehead, the arms of which tucked tightly into her pretty *coiffure*.

As she unbraided and combed my long hair, I sat upon a pillow on a low stool at her feet, tracing the multicolored needlepoint design on the cushion with my finger.

She found a snarl.

"Ouch!" I placed my hand on my head where it hurt.

"Sorry, *mon cheri*." She laughed lightly.

I glanced back. Her smile made her even more beautiful. Her eyes, blue like Gundred's, and her delicate chin and nose were perfect for a granddaughter of the King of France.

I rubbed the smart from the comb away and sat facing the flames dancing in the fireplace, counting each brushstroke. One hundred before bedtime each night was what my mother prescribed to achieve the desired shine.

"You're very quiet tonight," my mother remarked in English, her accent affected by her flowing French vowels.

She was right. I usually told her every detail of my day when I had her all to myself—which wasn't often. "*Maman*, may I ask you a question?"

"Of course," she said, giving my hair another gentle stroke. She kissed the top of my head.

I think she liked quiet times with me as much as I did with her. I didn't want to ruin tonight, but I needed to know something. "Did Gundred have to marry Geoffrey de Hussey because she was a pawn?"

"A pawn? Wherever did you hear such a thing?" *Maman* pulled lightly on my tresses until my eyes met hers. Her brows drew together.

"What I mean is, we must marry who we're told because of our nobility, correct?"

Maman loosened her grip, letting my head fall forward. "I suppose I can see the parallel, but I never thought of expressing it as being a pawn."

We sat in silence a moment as she combed.

"Were you a pawn, *Maman*?" I turned to look at her.

"With my first marriage." Her expression held a far-away sadness. "I was very young." Her greying golden hair reflected the warmth of the fire's glow, but her eyes held a shadow that worried me. "Still a child really, but my father was anxious for me to marry. Bishop Ivo contested the marriage since I was not yet twelve and the groom and I too closely related."

She was eleven? I swallowed hard. I didn't know that. She hadn't told me much about her first marriage, but I'd picked up some details from listening to the gossip of servants. "How closely related?"

"He was my father's first cousin. No matter. Father went over the bishop's head and petitioned Pope Urban, receiving a dispensation for the marriage." *Maman* pursed her lips, again reminding me there was something about her first marriage that she wasn't telling me.

I turned back to the hearth so she could finish her task, not expecting her to reveal more but secretly hoping she would.

She remained silent.

My questions were difficult to suppress. "Tell me again the man's name," I probed. For several moments I stared into the fire, waiting.

She pulled my hair into a ribbon atop my head. "The man's name was Robert de Beaumont, Count of Meulan." Her whisper held no affection. "He was forty years older than I."

Forty years. I held back a gasp because I wanted her to keep telling me her secrets. During their marriage she had borne him eight children, giving me many half-siblings. *She* had been a pawn too. I turned to look at her. "Was he . . . good to you?"

She bit her lip. "He treated me as would a stern parent, but he was considered by others to be a very wise man." She set the comb aside. "When the time comes, I hope your marriage will be happier than mine."

Her sadness pushed me to change the subject. I didn't want to admit I was sure I'd be just as unhappy as she had been. "But after he died, you married *Père* because you fell in love with him."

A radiant smile changed her face instantly.

The thought that my mother had married for love—even if only the second time—gave me hope. If I had to marry, could it not be for love, just as my parents? Why did they not want this for me and do all they could to achieve it? Then I remembered what Gundred had taught me. Women of noble birth are all pawns, used in the king's game of politics. I was now a woman and as such would be used to gain an advantage when trying to make a deal or an agreement.

Maman rolled my hair in a bun and secured it with a pin. In the morning, it would be unrolled to fall around my shoulders in soft curls.

I stood and faced her. "I want to be happy, *Maman.*"

She kissed both my cheeks and gave me an extra squeeze. "I pray you will find your way as I have. As Gundred has." Pulling away, she said, "Good night, *mon cheri.*" She left the room.

CHAPTER THREE

The next morning, I awoke before the sun. In the dark room, I took the time to snuggle into my blankets and remember the past days with Henry. I thought about playing chess with him and watching his strong hands move the pieces. Why did the man make me feel off kilter so often? I should not get my hopes up on marrying someone young. I remembered back to days before my sister Gundred's forced marriage to Geoffrey de Hussey, a man of fifty years at least. She had been only thirteen. And *Maman* only eleven when she wed, I now knew. I hadn't told *Maman* last night why I used the word "pawn." I'd first heard it when I was eight, right before Gundy's wedding.

Within days of guests arriving for her upcoming nuptials, the kitchen staff had already started preparations. The only good thing about Gundy's wedding was the food. The problem with us sisters being children of the wealthiest man in England and a loyal servant of our king was that we were expected to marry whomever we were told to, whether we loved that person or not.

I could still remember that day and the words said in private in the kitchen. My stomach had rumbled from the many wonderful smells of the wedding food, bringing me quietly there. I peeked around the corner into the large room of stone floors and walls.

With the servants outside plucking and preparing mallards, pheasants, woodcocks, and partridges, the room was almost deserted. Just Cook and his wife sat at the table cutting vegetables, talking softly, their backs to me.

"Stay out of their way, Ada," Gundred whispered, and I jumped. I hadn't realized she'd followed and stood just behind me. "They will not be in the best mood with all the extra work for my guests."

As usual, I ignored her.

Because she always strictly followed rules, she lingered in the doorway while I tiptoed toward the cooling pastries. I'd just take one. With their backs to us, Cook and his wife probably wouldn't even notice if I poked my finger into the bread pudding.

"The mistress wants many heavily spiced sauces and glazes. Everything must be precise," Cook said with determination. He wagged his head of grey hair covered partially by a white hat.

Behind them, I carefully lifted a pastry off the worktable. When no one called out to me, I snatched one more.

"French cuisine," his wife replied, waving her hand in the air. "Foul *and* rabbit smothered in almond gravy, no doubt."

"And pears poached in wine," Cook added. He complained often but I knew he was very proud of his cooking. Even though he was from Scotland, he cooked French food as if it were his native land. My mother insisted on her home cuisine.

As my soft slippers quietly brought me back to the doorway with a pastry in each hand, my mouth watered at the mention of the delicacies they discussed. French food was my favorite too. In the hall, I took a tiny taste of the bounty I'd stolen.

"All of this trouble for her little pawn," Cook's wife said in an odd tone.

Gundred's face drained of color, but she still snatched one of my pastries—the one I hadn't bitten into—then tears filled her eyes and she stormed away without a word.

25

Confused, I didn't follow her, but instead ran off to eat my sticky pastry in secret.

Later that afternoon, just when I thought she'd forgotten her promise to play chess, she finally came out of her room. She was the only one who spent time with me back then because my two older brothers thought I was too little.

After making yet another mistake during our game, I brushed the ivory chess pieces off the board in frustration and spun on my stool. "I'm too young to understand this game."

Gundred arched an eyebrow at me. "Eight is not too young." She bent down to retrieve the pieces. Her braid draped onto the floor, puddling at her feet.

I touched my own braid and frowned. Her dark blonde hair was more beautiful than my red. Crossing my arms, I turned away from her disapproving blue-eyed glare.

"I've told you, you must protect your queen," Gundred said, her voice soft but firm. "Remember that Razin said the queen is the most powerful piece on the board."

"Only according to *his* rules," I muttered.

My parents had welcomed the Moorish traveler into our home last winter, but he hadn't played the right way—the way we'd been taught. Razin claimed that we had changed the rules, not him. Chess had been in his country for centuries longer than in England.

I didn't want to play again, but I knew Gundred would make me.

Each piece clacked against the board as she replaced them.

Two years my senior, Gundy was determined to teach me everything she knew before she got married and left me. As the day approached, the gap between us widened daily. She no longer wanted to roam the hills and fields around our home. Instead, she spent more and more time with her friends and our servants, shuttered up inside our home.

I peered out the window and touched my nose to the glass. Early spring brought blooming blackthorn bushes and their tempting white blossoms. The children of the field workers already ran around outside in the distance, laughing and shouting. I should be outside with them—Gundred beside me.

"Are you ready?" she asked.

I pushed aside a lock of hair that had come loose from my braid before slowly spinning back to her on my stool. "It's my turn to go first."

Gundred nodded, her eyes never leaving the board.

I knew that look all too well. She planned her strategy before I even made my opening move. I bit my lip and looked at the board, giving up hope of ever being as smart as my sister. I reached for the pawn in front of my bishop.

We didn't speak until Gundred's knight took my pawn.

Trying to not show my surprise, I pretended I didn't care. "Oh, well. It was just a pawn."

"Just a pawn?" The unexpected quiver in her tone surprised me too.

"As you can see . . ." I motioned to the board. "I have plenty of them. I suppose one is" —I searched for a Gundy word— "dispensable."

My sister shook her head, her cheeks flushing pink. "We're not . . ." she began, then jutted her chin like she did when she was about to say something important. "It's unwise to discount the power of the one. Especially the one you think is small and weak. None are *dispensable*, Ada." Her eyes locked on mine. The fiery look she'd had earlier, after we'd overheard Cook and his wife, returned.

But why? Because they'd called Gundy a pawn?

She refocused her attention on the black and white checkered board.

I blinked slowly and made my next move. "What did she mean?"

Gundred didn't look up. "Who?"

"Cook's wife. Why did she call you *Maman's* little pawn?"

"Not just me." She pushed her bishop toward the center of the board.

I stared hard at my pieces. Not seeing any danger, I moved another pawn forward. "But wasn't she talking about the feast for your wedding?"

Gundred seemed to think about that carefully before answering. "She meant that you and I have a role to play." She swept her open palm over the board, drawing my eyes toward each chess piece. "It means that we are of noble birth."

This confused me. "The pawns are noblemen and women?"

She nodded.

That meant that not only were we pawns, but my father was one as well. That didn't make sense. As the Second Earl of Surrey, he was one of the wealthiest men in all of England. His riches came from my Norman grandfather's aid in battles with William the Conqueror. I pushed out my chest. "Sworn to defend and protect our king!" I reached my hand high, as if holding a sword.

Gundred grunted. "Among other *responsibilities*." Her voice trailed off as she made her next move.

Her wedding. "You mean marriage." My stomach flopped.

"*Oui.*"

I closed my eyes, hoping to block out the truth of it. "To someone you've never met."

"Not always but sometimes," she said matter-of-factly.

How could she accept her future so calmly? And mine? My eyes stung. "But why, Gundy? Why now? Why must you leave me?" I swallowed back tears.

She didn't look up. "Because my marriage to Geoffrey de Hussey is in the best interest of our family and our country. And I am ready."

If she was ready, why wouldn't she look at me? Was she hiding the truth from me? "But you're not even fourteen." Many girls married at thirteen, but some married at twelve. That was the legal age. I shivered.

She shrugged and briefly glanced up but not long enough for me to read her eyes. "I've spent every day of my life preparing for this. The things *Maman* has taught us—grooming, etiquette, taking care of a household—are to prepare us. We must set the example, Ada."

"Not I." I shook my head vigorously. I would only marry who I wanted, not some old man someone else picked for me.

"*Especially you!*" Gundred pushed her rook in line with my king. "With our nobility comes a great responsibility. We must rule equitably and lead and teach those less fortunate how to conduct themselves"—she paused, then said—"check."

My heavy bed curtains were pushed aside, bringing in sunshine and sweeping me away from my childhood memories. The morning rays shone onto the red, green, and gold tapestry hanging on the wall.

"Good morning, Lady Ada," Clare said. "Shall we prepare you for the day?"

CHAPTER FOUR

After a late morning meal in my bedchamber, I carried an altar cloth to the solar where I planned to embroider. I'd told *Maman*, although she wasn't pleased about my headstrong opinion, that seeing as women weren't allowed to touch the church altar, touching the cloth would be the closest thing to doing so. I supposed it was a way for me to resist precept.

My shoe heels clicked across the flagged floors until I stepped onto the carpet. This was the only fur carpeted room. The Great Hall was always covered in fresh rushes, however.

Sun streamed from tall, arched tracery windows lining one wall, facing the courtyard below. The room was the brightest in the castle and where *Maman* and I sewed daily with servants, two of whom sat near the far wall with tapestry frames in front of them, bent at their tasks.

They wished me a good morning, as I did to them, then I settled into my favorite cushioned chair in a corner by the window. Being French, *Maman* had decorated the room with furnishings of her country—tables with narrow, tapered legs covered in gilded gold and topped with marble, cupboards of intricately inlaid wood, and a House of Capet trunk inherited through her ancestors. The cushioned pieces were upholstered in deep blue. The heaviest piece in the room was a carved wooden chair where *Père* sat in the evenings.

I was not long at my embroidery before two muscular royal knights carried Henry in. He clasped white-knuckled to the chair he sat upon. They settled his chair near me. He smelled deliciously of cloves and citrus.

"Do you fare well, my lord? You look a bit terrified." I bit my lip to keep from laughing.

He raised an eyebrow and didn't catch the bait I'd thrown. "I'm going mad with inactivity."

I quickly tried to think of ways to distract him. When I got restless, I'd go for a walk. He couldn't do that. "Your knights carried your chair here, perchance they'd bring you outside?"

"To where and for what reason?" He frowned.

I'd never seen this side of Henry before. His sulkiness made him appear younger than the two and twenty I'd calculated him to be. The silence thickened around us as I stared at the massive stone fireplace. Above the large lintel a craftsman had carved our family crest of a knight's helmet crowned with a winged dragon. "I could show you Beatrice," I slowly said, and then wanted to kick myself for bringing up such a childish thing. Now who was acting young?

"Beatrice?" he asked, his brows low.

I shrugged. "Just a silly name for a weeping willow tree."

He laughed and I was pleased I had forced that melodic sound to spill forth.

"Gundred had chosen the name when we were children," I explained. "It's the largest tree on our grounds, and we imagined her a fairy queen, spending hours beneath her flowing hair."

He shook his head at me, but his eyes had brightened considerably from when he'd first entered the room.

I decided to let him in on another secret, hoping to continue our cheerful conversation. "After my sister married and left me as the only daughter in the home, I longed to be sitting across from her again—learning, listening, laughing. Instead, I found comfort nestling against the deeply furrowed bark of Beatrice's trunk, content to confide my deepest secrets to one who had the wisdom of age."

"Charming! And what's your relationship with Beatrice now?"

Dare I tell him I'd just visited her yesterday? *Non,* that would be revealing too much. I shrugged. "She's still enjoyable to sit under."

"Shall we, then?" he asked with a smile.

I put aside my sewing and stood. "I'll get the knights to come take you there."

Beatrice was quite a distance from the castle and the knights huffed and sweated as they carried Henry to her. Finally settled beneath her wispy boughs, I spread a blanket next to him to sit upon.

He straightened his leg, wincing in pain.

"May I comfort you somehow?" I asked.

"It helps to raise my leg. I should have asked for a cushion to be brought out with us."

"Here." I scooted closer and gently raised his leg, resting it on mine.

"Obliged." He smiled crookedly.

A late summer breeze rustled Beatrice's branches.

"Does not the tree's shelter have a feeling of a friendly canopy?" I asked.

"I can agree with that. I can also imagine a young, enraged redhead finding solace here. Better here than throwing rocks in the pond."

"I'd hoped you'd forgotten about that." My face heated.

"Was it really so hard to lose your sister?"

The kindness in his voice made me comfortable enough to share my memories, if only one. "I use her departure as a climactic time in the history of my life—there's before Gundy wed, and then there's after. I have not found anyone to replace her."

"I have felt that way about losing my mother," he said quietly, staring off toward distant hills.

My heart went out to him. "I feel ashamed for complaining about losing my sister to her husband. She is still alive after all. How long ago did you lose your mother?"

Henry forced a smile, as if trying to put me at ease. "'T'was not long after my return from King Henry's court. Her health had been failing for some time, so 'twasn't unexpected, but I don't believe one can ever be fully prepared for such a loss. Is Gundred happy?" he asked, choosing to change the subject.

I did not know him well enough to push him into talking about his mother, but I wanted to find out more. I found myself wanting to know Henry better. He was easy to talk to. Instead, I answered his question about Gundred. "The elderly man the king arranged she marry has since passed. She is now married to someone she loves—the Earl of Warwick. Her missives are filled with her joy and antics of her children."

"I'm pleased to hear it. Warwick Castle is quite a distance from here, however. Do you see her often?"

"*Non.*" I swallowed my sadness and decided I too would change the subject. "Do you ever feel enslaved to your responsibility as royalty?"

I expected a laugh or shrug, as was his nature, but instead he stared at me in a serious way. I tried to read his eyes. Had I insulted him? "What I meant to say, if you're like me, I would prefer freedom to choose what to do with my life." To give my heart to whomever I wished, I wanted to add but felt uncomfortable with the intense look he still carried.

"You want to choose marriage to whomever *you* want, I'm guessing you're saying."

I winced and picked at the blanket I sat upon. That's exactly what I wanted but I wasn't going to admit it to him.

He leaned back, locking his hands behind his head. "This is a hardship we have in common," he said looking toward the sky. "Being born into the families we are . . . well, it's a type of bondage, really. I don't think about it much anymore. I expect to be told where to live, who to war with, and who to love."

He looked at me then and my heart tugged in his favor. We did have this in common. I suddenly realized he may likely be lonely. Unlike me, he'd spent much of his life away from home, all for the sake of diplomacy. "You probably think me childish."

He shrugged. "Keep the childlike spirit in you alive as long as you can. There are many responsibilities ahead."

We spoke of less serious matters and laughed together until the knights came to carry Henry back to the castle.

I stood and brushed at my clothes then picked up the blanket. Before I followed the others, I strained to hear Beatrice whisper her opinion of Henry. But alas, she kept silent.

CHAPTER FIVE

I had a hard time concentrating on the mathematical lesson my old nurse placed before me. My father insisted I be educated since it likely I would be a nobleman's wife, "or a queen," he'd say with a wink. He sometimes threatened to send me away to a nunnery for my education, as he had with Gundred, but I begged him to not let it be so. I couldn't imagine being closed into small, dark rooms to learn of history, expenditures of households, and religion. For my sanity, I needed to get outside each day and wander the grounds of Reigate. Gratefully, *Père* understood my needs and pretended not to hear when *Maman* complained of him spoiling me.

I took a deep breath and pushed ahead, finishing my lessons two hours later. I set aside my tablet and daydreamed about Henry. I desperately wanted to be his friend and daily found myself searching him out since he couldn't easily come to me. *Would he come to me if he could?* I wondered. I hoped the friendship I felt for him would be reciprocated.

I said farewell to the nurse and went to the solar, but Henry wasn't there so I tried the Great Hall, but it was empty other than a male servant cleaning out the massive center hearth. Heading to the library, I realized this should have been the first place I searched because he loved reading, which was easily displayed in his intelligence.

When I entered, he looked up, excitement dancing in his brown eyes. "I'm reading a book by William of Malmesbury on the Antiquity of Glastonbury. It tells of the founding of the church at Glastonbury."

He acted as if he'd just told me his leg was healed and he could dance now.

"Sounds like something I'm forced to read as a history lesson." I shivered in mock distaste.

He gave me that crooked smile like he was oft to do when I spoke my mind. "Listen to this about St Philip," he said, and raised the book to read out loud. "I'll translate from the Latin it's written in. 'Desiring that the word of Christ should be yet further spread abroad, he chose twelve of his disciples and sent them to Britain to proclaim the word of life and preach the Incarnation of Jesus Christ, and on each of them he devoutly laid his right hand; and over them he appointed, it is said, his dearest friend, Joseph of Arimathea who had buried the Lord. They arrived in Britain in the sixty-third year from the Incarnation of the Lord, and the fifteenth from the Assumption of the Blessed Mary, and preached the faith of Christ with all confidence.'"

"I thought Christianity was brought to Britain by St Augustine in the sixth century," I said.

"That's just it. Disciples of Christ came almost five hundred years before that time. They came to Glastonbury. I had heard tales of this but have never seen it in writing. Fascinating, isn't it?"

I wanted Henry's good opinion but couldn't feign agreement. If I were Gundred I'd be at his feet begging him to read more. I smiled as unconvincingly as possible. "Fascinating," I said sarcastically, then immediately felt guilty for not having his enthusiasm toward the history of Christianity in England.

He lifted the book once again. "'The king gave them an island on the borders of his country, surrounded by woods and thickets and marshes, called Yniswitrin. Two other kings in succession, though pagans, granted to each of them a portion of land: hence the Twelve Hides have their name to the present day. These saints were admonished by the archangel Gabriel to build a church in honor of the Blessed Virgin. They made it of twisted wattles, in the thirty-first year after the Lord's Passion and the fifteenth after the Assumption of the glorious Virgin.'" He lowered the book again. "This makes me want to go to Glastonbury and have a look around."

"I did not realize you were a zealous supporter of Christianity." I settled onto a bench across from him.

"My grandmother and great-grandmother were faithful women at a time when the Scots did not care for such teachings." He looked away and colored slightly. "I have never mentioned it to others"—he cleared his throat—"and I wasn't being completely honest weeks ago when I told you that I don't think about my royal responsibilities as being a type of bondage. The fact that I'm told where to live and who to war with has kept me from my home and family. Being away from those I love for many years of my life, in my loneliness I often turned to God for solace. His Comforter has guided me and placed hope in my heart for a better future."

It was the most personal thing Henry had ever told me. He'd been used because of his lineage. I was moved by his sincerity. "I would like to have such a testimony of God. I believe you are favored."

"No more than the next man—or woman—who may ask God for guidance."

"I will endeavor to do so." I found myself wanting to get to know Henry better. Now that he'd opened up to me, perchance we could become better friends. "What are your hopes for Scotland?"

His mouth pulled down and I feared I'd made him sad. "My hopes are the same as my father's. I want our lands in Northern England restored."

"What lands are those?"

"Knowing how much you dislike history, I'm not sure where to start or how to explain without putting you in a foul mood." He cocked his head and smirked.

I raised one eyebrow. "Come now, I do like to learn of *living* people. Your father's life is not a history lesson."

He considered me then nodded, deciding to go on. "My father was the eighth son of King Malcolm, and the youngest born to Margaret of Wessex. He was still young when his father and brother were killed during an invasion of Northumberland. My father and his living brothers were too young to take the throne without a regent. Their uncle Donald made himself king and forced two brothers and my father into exile. They went to live at England's royal court in London. But my father's brother Duncan eventually fought for the Scottish crown and was killed. His brother Edgar was more successful and finally crowned King of the Scots. My father, still a young boy, returned to Scotland."

"That does not tell me what lands you want restored."

"As with all history lessons, there is much more to tell. I just wanted to make sure you were still paying attention."

I shook my head at him and laughed. "Go on."

"When the king of England died, his brother, Henry, whom I'm named after by the way..."

I rolled my eyes. Everyone knew that.

"King Henry took the crown and married my father's sister, Matilda."

"Ah, one of the many Matilda's. That's right. It's making sense to me now."

"You must listen better when tutored."

"Well, *oui*, I can agree, but don't tell my mother."

He chuckled and set his book aside, adjusted his broken leg on the cushion, then leaned back. "My father, a prince at the time, was given extensive territory south of the river Forth and became known as Prince of the Cumbrians. When he later married my English mother, he acquired a lordship scattered through the shires of Huntingdon, Northampton, and Bedford—all in northern England. There are many Englishmen who don't want a Scot as their lord, but these lands are my inheritance from my mother's family. Some wish it otherwise."

"The English lords and residents, I assume?"

"Correct."

"If I'm following your history correctly, your great-grandmother, grandmother, and mother were all from England. Are you really so Scottish?"

His expression of insult and astonishment made me titter. I shouldn't have, but I couldn't hold in my unladylike laughter and bent over in uncontrolled mirth.

I soon perceived I had been truly spoiled as the only daughter and youngest child left at home. Through serving Henry, I now realized how I enjoyed helping another in need. Over the weeks, he'd become homesick and perchance, although he didn't admit it, felt displaced. I could see it in his demeanor and had become familiar with his moods and mannerisms. On days when his mood was foul because of inactivity and impatience, I'd learned to allow him time. Or if I could not think of an activity, I'd cheer him by reading to him or deliberately losing at chess. I'd found through our friendship that I liked to serve others. And on that note, today I looked for something more to entertain a moody Henry.

An early autumn wind carried whispers of change through the stone corridors of Reigate Castle, and I rued the fact he wouldn't be with us much longer, for the bonesetter had said he'd be healed by autumn. I left the castle, heading toward the mews on the other side of the courtyard where *Père* worked with his falcons. I stepped into the cool stone structure with a high-pitched wood ceiling and waited for my eyes to adjust to the dimness.

"Good day, daughter. I've never seen you step foot in here before. And there's good reason." He chuckled. "Watch that the bird guano doesn't foul your hems."

I lifted my velvet skirt and scooted closer to where he stood holding a bird on his leather covered arm. Near the far wall my brothers and a knight worked with hooded falcons. Most of the birds roosted on beams, their beaks as sharp as a needle on the curved end.

I slipped on the guano, then thankfully righted myself. I looked at my shoes and grimaced, knowing Clare would not be pleased about cleaning my *poulaines*, then lifted my skirt higher. "Henry has often expressed his displeasure about how his infirmity keeps him from his favorite pastime of falconry. Knowing your falcons are highly trained and only taken on hunting trips past our deer park and into open lands where they can hunt small prey, I've come to ask your advice on how Henry could participate in falconry within our courtyard or closer to the castle."

Père's eyes widened. "My gyrfalcons and peregrines fly best when they are hunting. Just watching them fly is part of the sport and likely what Henry likes to see." He thought for a moment. "The birds have bonded with your brothers and me. But perhaps Henry would like to see our newly hatched young? If he's here long enough, he may see the fledglings take their first flight." He pointed to a nest on a niche where the stone wall met the wood rafters.

"I suppose it will have to do if you can think of a way to get him up those stairs to the nest. If not, can you conceive of another way to entertain him? I fear he'll leave within the fortnight."

Père shrugged. "We may be able to train some young ones in the weathering yard where he can participate whilst sitting in a chair?" *Père's* expression told me he wasn't sure that scenario would work either. "Birds of prey bond with their trainers. I'm not sure the young ones haven't already done so with the boys."

"How about we find out?"

"Let's give it a try this morning." He smiled at me tenderly. "You are a kind lass."

My face heated and I looked away. Did he know my feelings had grown toward Henry? He would not approve. "Obliged, *Père*."

I hurried back across the courtyard under grey clouds that threatened rain. Inside, I changed my *poulaines* to clean ones and then found Henry seated near the hearth in the Great Hall, his expression brooding like the stormy clouds outside.

With a courteous nod, I approached, my gown whispering against the cold stone floor. "How fare you this day, my lord?" I asked, but then regretted in case it made him have to face his foul mood.

"I curse the day I fell from my horse, if you must know."

I touched his sleeve. "It will soon be over." He probably felt relief in my words, but I only found sorrow in thinking of him leaving. "It's been an honor having you within our walls." My voice carried a warmth that defied the chill in the air.

He looked at me questioningly.

Embarrassed, I quickly went on. "A broken leg is a cruel fate, indeed. Perhaps there's something we can do to lighten the burden of your confinement?" I smiled playfully. "My father has asked if you'd like to help train some young falcons in the weathering yard today."

Henry instantly sat straighter, a wide grin on his face. "I regret I can do little but watch from a chair."

"*Père* thinks you may be able to do more."

"Ah, Lady Ada, if only I could fly them again. I miss the exhilaration of the hunt and the thrill of a falcon returning to my gloved hand."

"Shall I fetch the knights to carry you out?"

"Absolutely!"

In the days that followed, the castle grounds echoed with laughter and the flap of wings as my family, along with Prince Henry and myself, delved into the world of falconry. I truly loved all animals, these majestic birds of prey included. Despite his broken leg, Henry found joy in imparting his knowledge, while I proved to be an apt student sitting at his side. The affinity between us seemed to deepen with each shared moment, turning our falconry lessons into my cherished respite. I learned that the bond between falcon and falconer was a dance of trust and understanding.

I had a hard time not letting my feelings for Henry soar with the falcons. A one-sided bond wouldn't do. And the choice of my mate was not mine.

CHAPTER SIX

The flickering glow of torches cast dancing shadows on the tan and grey stone walls and colorful tapestries of the Great Hall. The light glittered from the armor of my ancestor who fought alongside King William the Norman. As a sacred memorial, the armor stood prominently against the wall, kept polished to a high shine.

As servants carried in food, the scent of roasted meats and fragrant herbs filled the air. We'd gathered around the dining table and *Père*, being the benevolent lord that he was, offered his hospitality by employing nightly minstrels for us to enjoy as we supped on stewed and tender pheasant, a pottage of mutton made with wine, herbs and spices, and all manner of vegetables cooked with cloves, currants, and dates.

Cook outdid himself when he proudly carried in *flambéed* plums and pears. All the dishes were a glorious end of summer reaping from our fields and groves.

Tonight, the entertainers played lutes, dulcimers, and harp, the gentle music a lovely culmination to an enjoyable day outside with Henry.

He and I had been spending hours together each afternoon. I felt as if I'd found a lifelong friend. I enjoyed helping him with tasks he couldn't perform because of his physical impairment. And he often made me laugh with his jests.

Instead of sitting to the right of *Père* as an honored guest, Henry sat at the opposite end of the table so he could turn to prop his leg on a stool. Consequently, he faced more toward me than *Père*. My two brothers sat on either side of the table, one near me, and one next to *Maman*, who sat resplendent in her rich silks and jewels, an air of grace and aristocracy about her. Sitting directly across from me, she kept a sharp eye on my face for some reason. Her mood appeared foul, and I didn't broach any subjects with her as we ate.

"Henry, shall we visit the mews again tomorrow? I hear the fledglings are trying to fly amidst the rafters," I said.

Maman tensed and before Henry could answer she said, "Ada, I feel you've been neglecting your *politesse* lessons of late." She raised a brow at me.

"Where have I failed in my courteousness, *Maman*?"

"You are to address our royal guest as Your Grace or Sire or My Lord."

I took a sip of mead to cover my embarrassment and gain time to think of what next to say. She was right. I'd become too familiar with Henry as our friendship had grown. I set down my goblet and swallowed hard. "Forgive my ill manners *Maman* and Prince Henry." I peeked at him. I often felt inexperienced and self-conscious about our age difference. He was ten years my senior and had lived at court and been tutored by the most astute.

He smiled crookedly and shrugged. "All is forgiven."

"*Oui*" was all *Maman* replied to me. Over the past weeks, she had rarely addressed Henry and continued with her sour disposition when around him, sometimes only speaking French, in which Henry wasn't fluent. Therein was another form of contention for her. *Maman* believed all nobles should speak French since most English masters did. Because Henry spent so much time at court, she felt he should know the common language there.

Maman continued, her French-accented English adding a touch of elegance to her words. "And I hope, Ada, you do not exhibit any inappropriate displays of familiarity with our Scottish guest."

My eyes met hers briefly, and confusion flickered within me. Inappropriate familiarity? What did she mean? I sensed she spoke as much to Henry as to me. "I assure you, I have been nothing but a friend to Henry . . . Prince Henry." My face burned and I bit my lip to stop it quivering. Did she not realize her insinuations humiliated me? Was *she* not displaying rude behavior?

I shifted in my seat, wanting to be anywhere but here.

Her eyes narrowed and she leaned toward me, responding in a hushed tone just as the minstrels stopped their tune, "Do not let your heart lead you astray." Because of the sudden dead silence in the room, she had said it loud enough for Henry and everyone to hear.

The servant behind her cringed.

Reginald choked a little on his food.

William rolled his eyes.

I wanted to crawl under the table. Before I could think of something to say, *Père* loudly cleared his throat. The tension around the table was palpable. I glanced at Henry.

His gaze had drifted to the flickering flames of the torches.

"I have hired a play performance for us this evening," *Père* said, trying to help me recover graciously, I was sure.

Reginald set down his spoon. "I hope it's the one about Daniel in the lions' den."

I lowered my gaze to my lap, fumbling with the edge of my linen napkin, an embarrassed apprehension coursing through me, but at least the subject of conversation had shifted. I didn't say any more throughout the meal and only nibbled at what was left on my plate, my stomach pinched and upset.

Finally, as the feast drew to a close, and *Maman* spoke with my father about the next day's activities, I leaned toward Henry and whispered, "I apologize for what my mother said. I hope you realize my actions have only been to help and entertain you during your infirmity."

He managed a small, if not disappointed smile, his eyes softening. "Your friendship is irreplaceable, Lady Ada. It means more to me than you know."

Relief washed over me as I realized that despite my mother's reservations, Henry valued our friendship as much as I did.

The tension between my mother and me remained unresolved, but in that moment, I knew that my loyalty to Henry was not misplaced. Our friendship would endure, even in the face of disapproval, and for that I was grateful.

He whispered, "I have something to show you after the play— up at the castle battlements. I'll have my housecarls take me up there. Do you think you can come?"

"I always have time to myself before Clare administers her evening *toilette*," I said quietly.

That night, before retiring to my bedchamber, I climbed the steps leading to the battlements. Coming outside to the castle's roof walkway, the heavy evening air smelled of woodsmoke, its chill catching me off guard. I wished I'd brought a cloak and hugged my arms around myself.

Henry stood alone at a distance, on his feet next to his chair, a red surcoat over his tan tunic. He leaned against the stone wall in front of him at a gap between the parapets. Past him and the swells of the green hills and dark forest beyond, the blue sky bruised with purple held one long cloud near its horizon. The bottom of the cloud reflected orange and yellow from the lowering sun. To have Henry in the same view of the land I loved caused a twinge in my chest.

I moved quietly along the *chemin de ronde*, wondering why Henry had asked me here. I was certain *Maman* would highly disapprove but seeing him on his feet made me realize our time together was likely drawing to an end and I did not care about her feelings at the moment.

As I neared, I spied Henry's two servants at a distance having a discussion amongst themselves and too far away to take notice of me.

Henry turned at my footfalls. "Ah, you made it." He stared back toward the exquisite sky. "I've been coming up here most evenings to watch the sunset and wanted to share something with you."

I stepped beside him, close enough to touch, but did not reach out, pulling my arms tighter about myself. It was the first time I'd been next to him standing. His height was several inches above mine and his shoulder width seemed larger than when he sat. Strange that his body was having such a pull on me. He was a robust knight. Power exuded from him in a rugged way. Reginald had told me stories of Henry's strength in jousting, yet all this time I'd been concentrating on his emotional needs. No wonder he was frustrated with inactivity. I took a deep breath and tried to stop thinking about his appealing shoulders, chest, and stature. "I am pleased you wanted to share whatever it is. Does it not hurt to stand on your leg?"

"Not much. I suspect it's time to remove the splints."

"I guessed as much." Did he too realize this meant he'd be leaving soon? Did it feel as bittersweet to him as it did to me? Surely his only focus was regaining his freedom.

The bottom globe of the sun touched the distant treetops.

"Look there." Henry pointed.

I followed his finger toward two birds flying our way, silhouetted against the apricot-colored sky. They circled each other in harmony, their expansive wings brushing against the night air, flying closer until they suddenly turned slightly and glided down, just below us. They were hawks.

I leaned out and realized a nest was tucked into the stone wall's ledge, not ten feet below.

Henry moved closer and pointed to the nest. "There are two eggs in there."

One hawk then two made their landing onto the nest. The sight of the majestic birds landing so close, unafraid of our presence, caused my heart to rapidly pound against my chest. "Glorious," I whispered.

Henry looked at me with tenderness, his eyes luminous to what we just witnessed. "Moments like these—our shared moments—have been a respite from the cares of my responsibilities. Your friendship is a treasure I hold dear." He spoke with a sincerity that stirred my heart.

My gaze met his, and in that glance, the unspoken depth of our connection hung in the air. He'd brought me here because he knew my love of birds. He reached out in goodwill as I had been doing for him. "Thank you for this gift. Our friendship is a testament to the beauty that can arise from unexpected bonds. Do not let my mother's words discourage."

"I didn't then, and I don't now." He turned back toward the horizon. "There are many at King Henry's court who don't like me for being a Scot. I do not let it change who I am."

"I am glad for it."

We stood quietly watching until the sun disappeared.

Henry breathed a sound of contentment. "In the quiet of the night we are forming a memory that I believe I'll never forget. I find myself drawn to you in ways words struggle to convey."

My heart quickened. "And I to you." Was this more than friendship then? I shouldn't let myself believe it could be. I would never be partnered with Henry by my parents' decision or the king's.

Henry nodded, accepting the weight of my words.

Our hands brushed against each other's, a silent acknowledgment of the intricate dance of emotions unfolding between us.

As Henry mended and could stand once again, we walked the grounds a little farther each day. When he felt up to it, we rode horses and practiced archery, never mentioning again our sentimental night on the battlement, and only acted as friends. I convinced myself I'd read too much into his words that night.

The cold of autumn settled in for good, and I willed the leaves to cling to their branches and not allow the wind and the season to carry them away. The clouds that had drifted in vibrant blue skies darkened each day with rain, making our excursions outside harder to come by until one day a retinue arrived to take Henry back to Scotland.

On the clear but chilly morning of his departure, he asked me to walk with him in the gardens. "I've enjoyed our time together, Lady Ada. I hope it won't be too long before we meet again." As we strolled, he took my hand and placed it in the crook of his arm.

I tried not to think about the tingles dancing through me from his touch. I looked away. The flowers around us had faded, their heads clipped, with some planters overturned completely, the soil dark in slumber, awaiting winter's frost.

Henry slowed his pace. "Our countries are not always at peace. Those northern lands held by England's king that my family would like to reclaim . . . well . . . I fear this may make our friendship hard to retain in coming years."

I was glad he put voice to our future friendship but worried he was right about our countries battling over land. I didn't want to lose him. I'd never had a closer acquaintance, other than my family members. "I will miss you."

Henry placed his hand over mine, then stroked it with his thumb.

A longing surged through me to lean against him. I fought the feeling and pulled my hand away. "Perhaps you should not touch my hand that way." I stopped walking and turned to face him.

He stifled a smile. "Perhaps not, but I did like it. I also like how you speak your mind."

I pulled in a breath of bravery to give him a little more of what was on my mind. "There is no future for us. You may have the privilege of choosing your wife, where I will have no choice. I will be given to whomever the king thinks best to serve his kingdom." My words were presumptuous, believing Henry had the same sentiments as me and would like to explore our feelings further. Having a romantic relationship other than friendship with him would only have to end in unmet promises, sadness, and pain.

Tears came and I turned away.

He stepped closer. "You're right. There are too many obstacles against us." His breath touched my neck.

I didn't want him to agree and longed for his hand again. If only I could lean back into his arms.

"I expect we can always remain friends?" His voice held hope.

I wiped away my tears and turned back, finding his eyes downturned.

It was best to end it this way, but my stomach felt sick and throat tight. I couldn't speak.

"I fear it's not only the king who would not have us wed," he said, glancing at me, then away. "Your mother barely shows me courtesy."

I was surprised my mother's treatment bothered him enough to mention. "*Maman?*" I still did not understand her coolness toward him. I should have questioned her but had kept my distance since the uncomfortable supper.

Henry turned toward his retinue in the distance. They were seated and ready to leave. "I must go." He turned back and looked me in the eyes. "If ever I see you at court, we must continue our friendship."

Dear Henry, I wanted to say. Instead, I put my hand on his cheek. I looked at his lips and he at mine.

He abruptly turned away. "Farewell, brave Ada, defiant speaker of truth, lover of birds and all things beautiful."

"Farewell, kind Henry, the man who makes me smile," I said through more tears. I spun away and walked at a clip to find a place of solace in Reigate's munificent countryside, my heart so pained I put my hand to my breast hoping for relief. But it would take more than physical pressure to heal it.

CHAPTER SEVEN

Anno Domini 1137
Reigate, Surrey, England

The year's end passed peacefully, with little excitement at Reigate Castle. With me soon to turn sixteen, *Maman*'s instructions in the arts of gentility and nobility became more frequent. I tried to apply her teachings, but my rebellious vein throbbed on occasion. I couldn't help feeling that nobility was a curse. My anxiety about my future grew. How soon would my parents tell me it was time— that they had chosen my husband? I had passed Gundred's age at her marriage.

She'd become a mother to an adorable son, Godfrey, and the very next year her old husband, Goeffrey de Hussey died. Gundred was shortly married again to Roger de Beaumont, Earl of Warwick, a much younger man. She appeared happy. But then again, Gundy would always make the worse situations into the best.

It had been on a drizzly morning when *Maman* walked into the solar with an air of determination. "Ada, put on warm clothing and your cloak. You're going into the village with me."

"*Moi?*" I looked out the window at grey, low-hanging thunderclouds and could see no reason to leave the warm fire.

And I wanted to finish the embellished hem I was embroidering. "But why, *Maman*? A storm may be upon us. With *Père* and William away, should we not stay in the safety of the castle?"

"Never mind the weather." She put on the cloak she carried. "We must visit one of our tenants. We'll take guards." She glanced toward me before pulling up her hood. " It's time you learn to extend a kind hand to the less fortunate. It's your duty as a noblewoman."

There it was again—the expectation, the duty that ran my life and kept me from having a true girlhood. I wanted to stamp my foot and refuse to leave but I had to do as *Maman* said. I retrieved my cloak.

"Lowly" was what Cook and others called the tenants we were to visit. They didn't learn French even though it was Frenchmen who ruled them. And here we were, nobles, going off to visit peasants.

Chadwick saddled our horses and four of our housecarls mounted to ride as protection. As women, we rarely departed from our property because of the English sentiment against the French ruling over them. Additionally, in recent months, bands of robbers—both native and foreign—roamed the land.

I mounted Cooper, whose golden mane was kept braided at my insistence. A bag had been tied to the saddle. "What are we bringing with us?"

"Provisions. We don't know what needs we may find."

Our guards rode both behind and in front of us. Moving slowly through meadow and woodland, I took in nature's beauty and smells. We passed wheat fields, flocks of sheep, a mill, and a small marketplace where vendors sold baskets, shoes, and other wares. The village of Cherchefelle with its diverse surprises was like another world from my castle life. In feudal pattern, the peasants worked one-fourth of their time on my father's estate and the rest on their own land to pay their rent to him each quarter.

Maman looked the other way as we passed a one-story building with a sign over the door that read, "Lulach Campbell's Alehouse." Men stared at us through half-glazed eyes. One man spat in the dirt. Our guardsman placed a hand on his hilt.

Months earlier, *Maman* tried to convince my father to shut down the alehouse because of questionable activities. Father had upheld the man's rights, and the tavern had stayed open. As we passed it, I tried with little success to keep my eyes focused ahead on the narrow dirt road.

Traveling a path through a thicket of trees, we soon arrived at a row of hovels made of stone and packed with earth. A few wooden animal pens stood alongside the road. Stenches from sewage and offal turned my stomach. A hungry looking dog weakly raised his head, stood and stretched, then limped behind us.

"This is the place," *Maman* said to Edmund, the lead housecarl.

The dwelling she indicated appeared in much need of repair, the doorstep a wooden box. A tattered blanket served as a door. I had always avoided this area and wished I wasn't here now.

Edmund helped *Maman* dismount. She untied the bag of provisions from my saddle. The other guards and I remained on our horses.

Neighbors came out of their dwellings, expressions of confusion on their work-worn faces.

Mud squished beneath *Maman's* slippers as she stepped to the hovel.

Glancing up, I willed the clouds not to open until we completed our task and returned to the safety of home. I shivered from the cold.

I expected *Maman* to leave the provisions on the doorstep, but instead she called out, "Greeting! Maggie, are you here?"

The cloth parted, and a young face peered out full of fear and suspicion. The girl could hardly be older than I.

"Dear God! Is that you?" *Maman* stepped closer. "Maggie, it is I, Lady Warenne."

I dismounted to stand in the mud. Breathing fetid air, I remained at Cooper's side.

The fear in the young girl's face softened as she recognized *Maman* and stepped outside with a curtsy. She tugged her shawl as if trying to hide her large abdomen. Her eyes passed over me to the guards still mounted.

I'd never seen such a pregnant belly on so young a person or a more pathetic-looking creature. Her tattered dress barely hung below her knees. Bruises covered her face and arms, and she wore rags for shoes. "Lowly" was confirmed in my mind, making me wish I hadn't come.

Maman offered Maggie the bag of food.

"Oh, Lady Warenne, you are most kind!" Moisture filled her eyes.

My mouth fell open. The peasant spoke as gentry.

Tears trailed down her dirty cheeks. "I've prayed for help. I feel so alone here."

I felt a twinge of compassion, but in my confusion, I pushed the sensation aside.

Maman put her hand on the girl's shoulder. "Word came to me of your troubles. I felt we should come to see how you're doing."

They put their heads close and spoke quietly.

I shivered and gazed longingly back down the road toward home.

Maggie stepped from *Maman*, staring at the ground. "Since my mother died . . ." A sob caught in her throat.

Maman surprised me by wrapping her arm around Maggie's grimy shoulders, encouraging her to continue.

The story spilled out. Five years previous her mother had died in childbirth along with the baby. "My father in his grief has lost our home and wealth—spending it on drink and I don't know what else. We've been living here for nigh on two years. He comes home drunk every night. One night he brought home a traveler . . . who . . ." She paused to control a sob. "Who forced himself on me.

55

Father did not protect me. He curses and beats me even when he's not drunk, but it's worse, so much worse, when he is."

How much of this could the neighbors hear? My face heated and I swallowed hard.

Maman peered into the shack. "Where is your brother?"

Maggie hugged herself. "John? He disappeared. He said he wanted to be anywhere but here." She looked at *Maman* with pleading eyes. "I have no one except Father." Her tears seemed never-ending.

I looked away from the anguish I saw written on her face.

"Maggie, get your things—if you have any," *Maman* said. "You'll come with us. You must not stay here another day."

My body went rigid. What was she thinking? Where was the nobility she'd taught me?

Maggie's brown eyes grew big. "But my lady! I cannot—"

"*Oui*, you can. I insist."

I suppressed a gasp.

Maman planted a fist on her hip. "You're going to have a baby— or babies, from the look of you—and you need proper care. After your delivery, you can work as a maidservant in my household."

My feet seemed stuck while I tried to understand. I gazed at the surprise on the neighbors' faces. None moved, waiting to witness what would happen next.

Maman motioned me forward. "Help Maggie collect her things."

My hand flew to my chest, and I looked to Edmund for help.

He bowed kindly and indicated the door with a gesture of his hand. No help would be coming from him.

"Be quick about it!" *Maman* ordered.

Terrified of what filth might lie inside, I timidly followed Maggie into the dismal one-room hovel. Two cots lined opposite walls. Other than a few pots and a fire pit, the room appeared nearly empty.

Not knowing what I was supposed to help with, I stood near the door while Maggie wept softly and pulled a few articles of clothing from a basket and put them onto the cot. After folding them carefully, as though they were her only treasures, she bundled them into a woolen bag. She pulled on worn slippers that looked once to have been grand.

Finally, with reverence, she knelt and slid a small box from beneath the cot and gazed at the contents momentarily. She stood and showed me a gem encrusted brooch inside.

How had she kept such an exquisite breastpin hidden from her father? "It's beautiful." I thought of the brooch on my mother's bureau I dearly coveted. Suddenly Maggie was no longer a ragged, pregnant peasant, but a girl my own age with feelings like my own. I grimaced inside as my guilt caused self-loathing. I dearly needed to improve my thoughts and emotions.

"It was my mother's," Maggie explained. "It's all I have of hers." She took the brooch out and rubbed it against her dress. "I didn't want my father to sell it for drink. He traded her other belongings, but I'll keep this forever."

Maggie tried to pin the piece of jewelry to her dress. Her hands trembled, and she lost her grip.

The brooch tumbled to the floor.

I hurried to rescue it. "Allow me to pin it on you."

She gave me a nod.

I eased the pin into the threadbare dress. "Come, Maggie." Gently I took her arm. "We'll help you through this."

She peered into my eyes. "How I appreciate you coming. You're as kind as your mother."

Now it was my turn to feel the sting of tears. Maggie had looked past my pride and had forgiven my arrogance. She'd accepted me as the noblewoman I should have been but was not. I decided then I'd become the person she thought I could be. I could do nothing less.

We exited the hovel.

Maman took the bag of food she'd brought for Maggie and handed it to another needy soul surrounded by several waifs. The dumbfounded woman proffered a curtsy of gratitude and uttered something ending in "m'lady."

Maman smiled and nodded back.

Edmund helped Maggie onto Cooper and then me in front of her. As we rode away, my initial feelings of repulsion toward the poor changed. I looked at their faces instead of their filthy clothing, at their eyes instead of their poverty. For the first time, I recognized that I had something in common with each person we passed. We were all human beings with similar needs. Amazed at *Maman* and her example, I was so grateful that she'd come to Maggie's rescue.

In the days that followed, Maggie and I worked together to find clothes she could wear before her delivery and appropriate maid's dresses to wear after. At first, she was quiet and reserved, but it didn't take long for her to become comfortable in my company. I was so very grateful for a friend after losing Henry. I soon told her about Henry and how I longed to see him again.

More of her story came out too. Her mother was of noble birth and someone *Maman* once knew. She'd married a Scottish commoner for love but upon her death, Maggie's father became a drunkard and gambler, losing Maggie's family home and possessions. Her brother John was thought to have traveled to Scotland to live with his father's family, but she was not sure.

It was fortunate we rescued Maggie when we did, for the wait was not long. In less than two weeks Maggie went into labor.

I was not allowed at her bedside, only *Maman* and a midwife she'd hired. I paced the floor in the next room—praying, listening, anxious each time I heard her cries. The relief could not have been sweeter when I heard newborn cries.

I overheard the midwife talking to *Maman*. "If you had not brought her here when you did, she would have died alone—the babies too. Sadly, birthing these twins ruined her for bearing more, poor dear."

Maggie's recovery went slowly. I visited her bedside daily and she welcomed my company, allowing me to help with the twins. I offered to teach her French, and she readily accepted.

Maggie's rescue sparked a change in my heart. I liked having the power to change someone's life. It gave me a sense of fulfillment.

I watched everything my mother did after that. She often took me to deliver food baskets to the needy or sent servants to do the task. It seemed she constantly looked to meet the needs of others, and she did it with kindness. Her example deepened my own desire to serve.

One afternoon, I came into the kitchen and found my mother dressed to go out.

"Take care, m'lady," Cook said, handing over a basket of baked goods.

"Do you want company today, *Maman*?" I asked.

"I'm afraid I don't have time to wait for you to change," she replied. "A regiment of the king's soldiers are encamped just outside of Cherchefelle. I hope to add a little cheer to their ranks before they depart."

She smiled and kissed my cheeks before slipping out the door.

"Lady Warenne is much like Queen Margaret," Cook said, still watching the door.

"Queen Margaret?" I asked.

"Aye." He turned from the door to a pot of stew simmering over the fire. "The former queen of the Scots. She was very charitable, giving alms to the poor, feeding the hungry."

I couldn't help smiling—swelling with pride that my mother would be compared to a great queen—but perhaps more so that it would be the Queen of Scots. Henry's relations held special interest for me even though I'd been desperately trying to forget the way he'd made me feel.

"How do you know Queen Margaret?" I asked.

"I didn't *know* her. Queen Margaret died when I was a lad, but folks talked about her kindness long after she was gone. The Scots nobility had always been unrefined and lawless, and we'd all listen to stories from travelers with keen interest of how she might have changed them."

I didn't like hearing disparaging remarks about the Scots. Henry had not been unrefined in any way. But Cook reminded me of when Henry spoke of his Christian mother and grandmother. Queen Margaret would have been his grandmother. "I've heard it's very beautiful in Scotland."

"Aye, I should love to visit again if 'twasn't so far."

"I also would like to visit the land of the benevolent Queen Margaret of Scotland," I mused, somewhat dreamily.

"Perhaps one day you shall."

CHAPTER EIGHT

Anno Domini end of 1137- 1138

A fresh dusting of snow covered all of Reigate and Churchefelle in mid-November when *Père* was called to King Henry's bedside. *Père* was with him when he passed. News spread quickly that England's king had died.

I waited with great anticipation for news of the succession. Mounting tension on the subject had me deeply concerned about Prince Henry's vow that his father would support and uphold King Henry's wishes that Empress Matilda be crowned. When the king's nephew, Stephen de Blois, stepped in and took the throne before King Henry's daughter could arrive in England from France, I feared our two countries—Scotland and England—would go to war.

"'Tis for the best. A woman is not fit to rule," my brother William said after returning home from the coronation. "Blois will make a better king."

I turned to *Père*. "Is this how you feel too? Is it true that a woman is not fit to rule?"

Père touched my hand tenderly, but his eyes gave away that he was caught in a trap. "Women do not lead armies or fight in wars,

61

but I am sure we will discover how powerful Empress Matilda can be if she retaliates. I believe she will not let the usurpation of the throne pass without a fight."

"If she had not married Geoffrey, count of Anjou, rival of the Normans, I'm sure many nobles would not be against her," William said.

My fear over *Père's* prediction of Empress Matilda's retaliation was immediately overshadowed by King David of the Scot's directing attacks in Northumbria. Prince Henry's assurance of his father's loyalty to King Henry and Empress Matilda had been deadly accurate. King David also saw the unrest as a chance to expand his territories and claim as heritage for Prince Henry lands once belonging to his mother, Matilda of Senlis. I worried the prince led the Scottish armies with his father.

Père and my brothers prepared to join forces with those of King Stephen when called upon. My family would be on the opposite side of Prince Henry. I prayed it wouldn't happen.

One blustery afternoon in late January, a messenger arrived.

I lurked in the corner of the Great Hall, listening with dread. Would *Père* leave the warmth of Reigate to fight against Prince Henry and his father?

"Carlisle, Alnwick, Norham, Newcastle, and Wark have all fallen into the hands of King David," the breathless rider said, handing my father a parchment emblazoned with King Stephen's seal.

Père opened the message and frowned.

"Must you go?" *Maman* asked.

"Aye, but not as I had expected." *Père* set the parchment aside and took my mother's hands. "Trouble is stirring in Normandy. King Stephen is sending me and the boys to defend Rouen."

"I hate to see you go but at least you're not fighting the barbaric Scots."

Instant relief swept through me. *Père* and my brothers would still be fighting, but somehow knowing they would not be doing battle with King David's troops calmed my heart. When *Père* had gone to war before, it had always been against faceless, nameless enemies. Now this new enemy had a face I couldn't seem to put out of my mind. And he was not barbaric at all.

For the next two months, I spent hours in our little chapel, praying for not only the men of my family in the south but for Henry in the north. I could not tell if God heard my pleas because I didn't receive an answer. I tried to have the faith of Gundred and also find the comfort Prince Henry said he'd received from prayer. I didn't give up trying and finally felt a sense of relief, taking away my deepest worries. I vowed to never step away from God again.

We received occasional news from *Père* but heard little about the Scots.

I couldn't help but wonder if William was wrong. If a woman did lead the kingdom, would she not be more inclined toward peace? I knew I would be. I would do all in my power to stop the killing.

Maggie became an almost constant companion and a vital distraction while *Père* was away. As she learned French to communicate better with *Maman* and other members of the staff, I took to studying English and Scottish history more seriously. Maggie helped. She'd not only become my confidant, but knowing my concerns about Henry, she found a way to bring back news from the village of what was happening in the North.

One day she said, "They're saying King Stephen led his army to meet King David at Durham. 'Twas to be a terrible battle."

"'Was to be?'" I asked. "Did they not fight?"

Maggie shook her head. "They've reached a treaty. Praise be to heaven."

A treaty. The words were music to my soul. Perhaps without the support of her uncle King David, Empress Matilda would give up her claim to the throne and *Père* and my brothers would come home.

By late spring, they did return. Troubles in Normandy were somewhat subdued, though none could say for how long.

CHAPTER NINE

Anno Domini Spring 1138

"Oh, to think I know someone who has an invitation from the king!" Maggie held up one of my tunics. "You must take this one. The green matches your eyes perfectly." She carefully folded the garment and placed it into my traveling chest.

It was to be my first time attending a celebration held by King Stephen. Having passed the sixteenth anniversary of my birth, I was grateful to have heretofore escaped the fate of an early marriage, but I feared that my time was soon at hand. "It seems curious that my name was included on the invitation, does it not?" I asked. Was the king calling me to him to tell me whom he'd chosen for my husband or could it be he wanted to examine my appearance and temperament?

"Your brothers now attend court, why not you?"

William and Reginald, along with *Père*, were frequently visitors to King Stephen's court. The year before, William had become a great supporter after the king had pursued him and other young nobles as they fled the battle in Normandy. The king did his best to pacify them rather than make them fight. To prove himself loyal, William had become the strongest and bravest knight in the kingdom. No one had unseated him in jousting.

"But why now?" I wondered aloud, fearing I knew the answer to my question.

"Impossible to say." Maggie hefted my traveling chest onto the bed. "But to stay at Westminster Palace! I can only imagine the splendor."

I shrugged, entirely uninterested in experiencing the grandeur. "At least Gundred will attend too. Oh Maggie, she seems truly happy with her husband." I handed her another pair of slippers.

In her last letter, Gundred had written that Roger had proved to be a doting father to young Godfrey and their new daughter, Gundred. Gundy was now pregnant with a third. She said Roger was a kind and good soul and especially generous to the poor.

I frowned, watching Maggie pack my new tunics into the chest. "What if the king is eyeing me for an old goat?" My stomach turned nervously at the thought of what might await me in London.

"Goat?" Maggie scrutinized me suspiciously.

I'd often expressed my dread to her of an arranged marriage. "Do you think this could be my time to be married off to an ancient earl who will expire within a few months?"

Maggie grinned and covered her mouth to suppress a laugh. "Oh that kind of goat! Pah!"

Père had ordered our gilded cart readied for our trip from Reigate to London. I settled inside with *Maman* and William's new, quiet, and petite bride Adela. She knew little English and could converse with only those who spoke French. *Père*, William, and Reginald, along with the housecarls, rode horseback at our front and rear. *Père's* blue-and-white checkered flags and livery presented a glorious tribute.

We moved northward through verdant countryside, along well-traveled paths. Late in the day, upon passing a few taverns on the outskirts of London, enticing aromas greeted us. My mouth watered after a long day of travel. "What do you think they're cooking that smells so delicious, *Maman*?"

"Perhaps"—*Maman* inhaled deeply—"roasted lamb with rosemary."

I only hoped that whatever we'd eat at the palace would be as delicious as the lamb smelled.

Dolefully, when we entered the city, the smells changed drastically.

Adela coughed and covered her nose.

I attempted to block the stench with a cloth and focus instead on the bustling commerce and vehicles and the maze of twisting streets and lanes lined with shuttered houses whitewashed with lime. I'd never seen so many people in one place.

After crossing the river Thames by bridge, every road came alive with vendors selling goods and shoppers filling the streets. The sounds thunderous compared to the country, I would have loved to linger, looking over wares and listening to minstrels playing their instruments. The lively music enticed me to dream of a different life than my sedate existence at Reigate Castle. Were it possible to escape the cart undetected, I would have become lost in the crowd. But alas, my fate awaited, and the cart pushed onward.

"There it is. The Palace of Westminster." *Maman* squeezed my hand.

Adela and I leaned toward the window.

I hadn't realized I trembled until then. Despite my hesitation over what lay ahead, the palace's magnificence along the riverbank left me breathless. The spiral towers stretched higher than any other buildings. The palace stood surrounded by perfectly sculpted shrubbery and vibrantly colorful flowers that made it seem we were entering another world altogether.

"*Magnifique*," Adela said.

Our entourage led us to the front entry, where we were greeted by men in the king's livery of blues and reds. They wore red-and-white striped stockings under knee-length tunics and capes decked with gold tassels.

An attendant took my hand as I descended from the cart. "Welcome, my lady." He bowed low.

As a group, we were escorted into the palace.

Inside I could scarcely take it all in. The splendid tapestries, massive furniture, and spacious halls dwarfed the comforts I'd become accustomed to. "I can never imagine myself living in such a place," I said under my breath.

"There's little reason to imagine it," *Maman* replied, standing much closer than I had realized. "Rather, you should prepare yourself. These displays of riches are just as splendid in France."

My heart stilled. Part of me longed to ask her what she meant or if she'd been discussing my marriage with *Père*. But I preferred to live in ignorance as long as possible. Once I discussed my marriage it might make unwanted events unfold.

We settled into our rooms, and almost immediately the door flew open and Gundred rushed in with her husband Roger and their children.

I hurried into her arms. "I have missed you so!" An embrace by Gundred was like being accepted completely, her love unconditional.

"And I you. Gratefully, we will have weeks together here." She pulled back, keeping hold of my arms. "You must fill me in on everything you've done these last years."

We laughed, knowing that was impossible. Yet the passing of time did not change our affection for each other.

Père and *Maman* moved in to take her from me and I had to give her up. But only for a time. As she said, we had weeks to visit.

After they left, *Père* asked if I wanted to visit Westminster Abbey. I readily agreed, always happy to be alone with him.

Near the palace, I gazed in awe at the abbey's high arches. They seemed almost to reach the heavens. Inside, lavish stonework in the Great Hall was punctuated with ornate, stained-glass windows, each telling a story.

"This abbey was built roughly around a hundred years ago in 1040," *Père* said, by the Saxon King Edward, later known as Edward the Confessor. It was built as a monastery known as West Minster.

Pere stopped strolling and admired an artist's depiction of William the Conqueror at the Battle of Hastings.

I came up behind him and gently laid my hand on his elbow. "Do you commend the representation, *Père*?"

He nodded. "He was crowned king here on Christmas Day over a half-century ago."

"William the Conqueror?" I knew the history but wanted him to continue.

"Aye. When Edward the Confessor died without a male heir, many claimed the crown, but it was this battle that put William on the throne. My father fought alongside him, and his loyalty won him the title Earl of Surrey."

I'd never considered how divided the people must have been at the time—perhaps very similar to what we were experiencing now. I wondered what my father's loyalty to King Stephen would win him. "Were you at the coronation?" I asked, slipping my arm through his.

"Nae, my child. That happened long before I was born." He gazed toward the altar. "But my father was here. He said it was quite chaotic, being spoken in both English and French."

I could well imagine it would be difficult for any overpowered people to subject themselves to their conqueror, but the language barrier further complicated matters. "Didn't you once tell me that when those inside the abbey shouted their approval, the Norman guards outside supposed William had been assassinated?"

"They set fire to buildings around the abbey. The church filled with smoke, the congregation fled, and riots broke out"—*Père's* chuckle was filled with more ire than mirth—"and yet William and the clergy completed the ceremony despite the bedlam around them."

I couldn't imagine it. "How did they maintain the peace enough to finish?"

"Peace is never easy to maintain." He brushed his hand affectionately under my chin and placed his arm around my shoulders. "But do not underestimate your importance in helping to achieve and maintain it."

I didn't understand what he meant. *Père* had made it clear that women did not belong anywhere near the field of battle. "How would I ever help achieve peace?"

"I cannot speak of it yet but just remember that sometimes it takes only a few people to bring peace among nations—people who are ordained of God and have a pure heart—like you."

His words overwhelmed me, but I did long for peace with Scotland. I doubted someone as obscure as me could help that come to pass.

The faraway look in his eyes dissuaded me from asking more questions.

I leaned against him. *Maman* had told me that men who lived through battle—and witnessed blood and torn bodies, killing and death—were changed men. My father was repeatedly haunted by bad dreams. Often gruff and somewhat hard around the edges, he could still be exceptionally tender. Other soldiers had become calloused from the same adversities. Perhaps being in this sacred building with its history and memories softened him.

That evening in the palace, I stood between *Maman* and Gundred as *Père* and Roger introduced us to many dignitaries. Several wore long robes—the *pelisse* so favored in London—and ribbons and medals of honor hung from them, adding to the splendor of the occasion.

I wore a dark green tunic with silver thread embroidered at the hem and along the edges of trumpet sleeves that hung low, covering my hands. Surveying the room for the face of my future husband, I felt almost faint. I loathed old men's stares, fearing they might be evaluating me as a possible bride because of my mother's lineage and my father's wealth. "Pawn" echoed in my head. Would my husband be ancient like Gundred's first husband or young like Roger or perhaps somewhere in between? Could he be a great warrior, like my father?

"Hold still," *Maman* whispered in my ear. She pushed up my sleeve and took my hand.

"Forgive me, *Maman*." Looking around the Great Hall, I tried to stay calm.

Wreaths of multi-colored flowers decorated the room. Long tables lined the walls, brimming with dishes of fine foods, like white cheese covered with fennel seeds and strawberries. My mouth watered at the chicken, venison, and fish set out on large platters. Pastries of every kind, including custards and fruit pies topped with smaller pies to represent crowns, appeared so delicious. Pewter plates had been stacked next to mugs filled with ale and wine.

Trumpets sounded, drawing our attention to the double doors at the far side of the hall. A majestic procession entered the room with King Stephen and his wife, another Queen Matilda, regally in front.

One face among the procession immediately made my heart quicken. Prince Henry followed the king. The treaty Maggie had spoken of had truly taken effect or else the two royals would not enter together. I had not expected Henry to be here, and the realization caused my knees to shake. I wanted to run to him but kept still, as a noble woman should.

From across the room, his gaze met mine, and that familiar, mischievous smile crossed his lips.

I lowered my eyes and whispered nervously, "*Maman*, Henry is here."

"His Royal Highness, Prince Henry," she corrected.

"I'm astonished he has come to court so soon," whispered Gundred from behind us.

"His father's treaty requires him to pay homage to King Stephen," *Maman* replied. "His title and lands have been restored. Now it is up to him to restore the goodwill that once existed between our countries. He has much to overcome."

"What do you mean, *Maman*?" I remembered how Henry had told me he'd been taken from home countless times before. Now he's used as a hostage in a treaty, sent to an English court to live. My heart went out to him, and I hoped he wasn't lonely as he had been before.

"His ancestors were barbaric, uncivilized, and unrefined," *Maman* stated quietly with no affection.

Her disparaging remarks were unlike her. After Henry had left our home, *Maman* had told me emphatically that she would not want me married to a Scot. As good as her heart was, she did not have kind feelings toward a whole country of people. It puzzled me. Henry served Scotland by spending time at the English court. His time and service given to service should be honored. Was I the only one who knew how this sacrifice must be wounding him?

"Come," *Père* commanded, taking *Maman*'s arm. He motioned to Roger, Gundred, and me. "We must greet King Stephen."

Maman slipped her arm around my waist and whispered pleadingly, "I entreat you, Ada, remember what I've taught you."

Upon reaching King Stephen, we stood waiting while several people ahead of us were presented. Only a few feet away from Prince Henry, I dared not look in his direction. I already felt the heat rushing to my cheeks thinking about our last conversation at Reigate. I had been very blunt to speak of marriage. We both knew it could not be.

So strange to think we were now at court, though with an unexpected king on the throne and under different circumstances than I had imagined. Would Henry remember the promise he'd made to be my champion?

Finally, our turn came. *Père* stepped forward.

"How are you this fine evening, Earl Warenne?" King Stephen greeted. He was a thin man with close-set eyes, about forty, but not yet grey.

"I fare well, Your Majesty." *Père* turned to *Maman*. "You know my wife, Elizabeth of Vermandois, Countess of Surrey. May I also have the pleasure of introducing my daughters, Ladies Gundred and Ada. I assume you know Gundred's husband, Roger de Beaumont, Earl of Warwick."

Maman, Gundred, and I curtsied deeply.

"Of course." King Stephen nodded and gestured toward the young man beside him. "This is the Earl of Huntingdon, Henry Mac David, Prince of Strathclyde, an ally." He chuckled as if it was a jest. "A *conquered* ally, that is. He is here to pay me homage."

My eyes shifted to Henry.

He ignored the verbal stab, bowing to my mother and Gundred, then to me. Our eyes met—his brown and penetrating in interest. It seemed he wanted to say something to me.

Feeling vulnerable, I glanced away.

"We've already met," Henry said. "I'm most pleased to renew our acquaintance."

"We are most humbled that you remember your visits to Reigate, Your Highness," my mother said.

"Your *hospitality* left a lasting impression on me." His sideways glance, coupled with his broad smile, assured me that he remembered every detail of his time at Reigate, including *Maman's* coldness.

Another family of nobles stepped to the king, introducing their fair-haired daughter, but Henry's eyes were clearly fixed on me.

I couldn't help but return his smile before casting my eyes downward.

Maman appeared troubled, squeezed my hand, then turned to converse with the queen, pulling me away from Henry.

Another young woman was brought forward and presented to the king—this time a tall beauty in a blue velvet tunic. Silky black hair cascaded down her back.

King Stephen leaned toward Prince Henry, engaging him in the conversation.

Henry smiled pleasantly at the young woman and her parents.

I clenched my teeth and folded my arms, turning away, not wanting to see any more of the interaction between Prince Henry and the beautiful woman.

The king's cackle filled the hall, and I looked back.

Color had drained from Prince Henry's face.

I felt overwhelming sympathy for him. I never imagined that he may face the same trouble at court as I. The king could choose the prince's fate too.

I stepped away from my parents.

"The king seems determined to antagonize him," Gundred said, seeming to read my thoughts.

"I don't understand why," I replied.

Gundred said near my ear, "Roger told me, had the king not been battling Empress Matilda in Normandy, he never would have agreed to King David's terms. He means to make Prince Henry suffer for the lands he lost in the treaty. Although, King Stephen promised if he ever chose to resurrect the defunct earldom of Northumberland, Prince Henry would be given first consideration."

I was sure this was what Henry wanted. More than ever, I longed to possess the wisdom and discernment of my older sister. "The chess board doesn't have a prince piece," I observed.

"He is very much a pawn in the king's game, until he becomes a king himself."

CHAPTER TEN

The banquet of opulent foods in the Great Hall at Westminster Palace was just as I had dreamed, but I'd failed to imagine how loud it would be. With timbers reaching to high ceilings, the voices and the clattering spoons on pewter plates seemed to vibrate and clash in the air.

Introduced to so many noblewomen and men, I couldn't remember all their names. *Maman* would not be happy and would likely add more peerage into my lessons. I looked about to all those seated within the u-shaped table arrangement and silently repeated what names I could remember. Many were young noblewomen about my age.

Longing for a friend, I wished to talk with them.

They in turn watched me. Perhaps more so because my family had been honored to sit with the king and queen. My mother's older sons from her first marriage to Robert de Beaumont were with us—Robert the Second Earl of Leicester, who was considered a great supporter of King Stephen, and Waleran his twin, First Earl of Worcester, who'd recently become one of the king's top advisers.

King Stephen had announced earlier in the day that my brother William would accompany his half-brother Waleran on an embassy to Paris for the purpose of ratifying a treaty between the English and French kings. *Père* had told us before supper how pleased he was that William had become a man of influence, trained to serve the people. He was now famous for his chivalry and competition as a knight as well.

The Beaumont twins rarely visited Reigate. They'd grown up in King Henry's court after their father died and my mother and father married. They were only two of my twelve siblings. With me at the tail end of the family, it didn't feel like I was one of so many.

Prince Henry sat to the king's right with my father to the left of the queen. Each time I glanced in Henry's direction, I caught his eye. He appeared perfectly relaxed and enjoying the evening, whereas I felt a bundle of nerves.

"You were a guest at Reigate Castle, cousin? I must say that I envy you." The new Queen Matilda—a third Matilda, another cousin to Prince Henry, and also the wife of King Stephen—leaned around the king to address Henry, then smiled at my mother across the table. "I have yet to accept an invitation from the lovely Lady Warenne, though she has graciously extended several."

"I do hope that peace will triumph, and you may soon enjoy a visit," *Maman* replied, coloring slightly.

"Your twin sons speak of Reigate's beauty often. And this enchanting creature"—Queen Matilda reached across the table for my hand—"I've heard much talk of her. Especially that of her exceptional beauty."

It was impossible to suppress the heat that rose to my cheeks. *Exceptional beauty?* Had my half-brothers been speaking of me so? It was difficult to imagine them expressing fondness, for they barely knew me. I glanced to Waleran on my left.

He shrugged his shoulders as if not knowing who gave such a compliment.

"You are so kind," *Maman* said, nudging me.

Suddenly alerted to the fact that I had left an uncomfortable silence, my face burned hotter. "I . . . um . . ." My mind went blank. "*Merci,* Your Majesty."

The chatter in the crowded Great Hall and the clank and clatter of dishes, but mostly the nearby presence of Henry, overwhelmed my nerves.

Several moments went by with *Père* in deep consultation with the king, the queen nodding in agreement to whatever they discussed.

I caught only snatches of their conversation with the growing din of the servants making their way to the tables with horns of mead and wine.

Suddenly, King Stephen's clear voice rose above the din. "I'm afraid King David's word means very little to me without his son's presence here to assure his loyalty."

Prince Henry pulled back his shoulders. "My father's loyalty should cause you no concern, Sire, with or without my presence at court."

The king flourished his hand dismissively, each finger brandishing a large jewel in gold. "Nevertheless, I must insist on sealing the treaty. You shall take an English bride before the spring's end."

Maman's eyes turned sharply on me as if willing me to do or say nothing.

I glanced around the hall, noting how strikingly similar everyone suddenly looked—all nobles with eligible daughters. The reason for my invitation, for my presence at court became clear. My heart pounded deafeningly in my ears. Did *Père* know? Surely *Maman* did not. It was likely I was the only one whose mother didn't like Prince Henry.

He sat silently staring at his plate, face flushed, demeanor changed entirely. "I should think such dealings would be better discussed privately, Your Majesty."

The king laughed. It was not a pleasant sound—almost like the cackle of a chicken. He appeared to revel in the prince's discomfort.

"Should we not enjoy this sumptuous repast, Sire?" *Père* mercifully suggested. He looked at me and winked.

The king peered down his nose at Prince Henry for a moment longer before acquiescing to my father's suggestion.

Maman leaned close. "Where has your tongue been tonight?" she whispered.

"My tongue?"

"You didn't say a word when introduced to Prince Henry, and then nothing to acknowledge the queen's compliment."

"Forgive me, *Maman*."

"At very least, you could have exchanged pleasantries, as you've been taught. As it is, you've left the impression that you are entirely mute when we know the opposite is true. And here I thought you'd speak your mind, as you do at home." *Maman* took a drink from the goblet in front of her.

"Perhaps Lady Ada made more of an impression than you think," Queen Matilda chimed in, her hearing obviously sharp. "The prince cannot take his eyes from her."

Maman and I both looked down the table to where Prince Henry sat.

Maman harrumphed so quietly I was sure I was the only one to hear.

He still stared at his plate, brows together. He was not looking at me now at all. Was it really such an uncomfortable idea to him that he marry an English woman? Or was it because he did not want to wed someone he had not chosen?

The queen, *Maman*, and I eventually conversed at length about Reigate and then she told us about her rewarding work with the Knights Templar. I found I liked her very much and wished I had such a friend here at court that was my own age.

When she and *Maman* continued the conversation about a favorite chateau in France, I was left to my own thoughts and the

78

delicious feast spread before me. After so many years of anticipation about marriage, I felt a strange tangle of emotions. Would the king really consider me as Prince Henry's wife? Could *Maman's* distaste of the Scots discourage the union? I seriously doubted my mother would ever tell the king her opinions. She'd been raised to honor her sovereign, as she'd taught me. But she'd surely already voiced her opposition of the match to my father, and it appeared he had the king's ear. I feared hoping I could be Henry's match. I'd always thought I was destined to marry an elderly man. If I was chosen and Henry felt forced to marry me, then what would I do?

I'd never dared to dream that someone as young and handsome as Prince Henry might be chosen for me. Just looking at him gave me such a mixture of pleasure and pain—a flutter in my stomach that turned to an ache.

CHAPTER ELEVEN

The next two days were a blur of activity at the palace—walks in the gardens, musicians in the hall, and decadent meals. Maggie took special care to make sure my hair had been arranged perfectly each morning before I left our chambers, and for the first time in my life, I didn't protest.

I found myself searching for the prince in every room we entered. I was both relieved and disappointed when I couldn't find him. I assumed that we would eventually have an opportunity to speak to each other again. I hoped to make the next interaction more lighthearted than our last conversation.

In crowds, Henry often appeared late and withdrew early, always surrounded by people. It seemed difficult to even catch a glimpse of him, and my parents made no attempts to approach him.

It wasn't until after the dancing began on the third evening that I saw him coming toward me from across the Great Hall. I could barely breathe.

"Lady Ada de Warenne." The prince took my hand and bowed.

Slowly, with deliberate composure, I curtsied and smiled. "Your Royal Highness." I'd never been so grateful my tunic covered my trembling legs.

"May I have the pleasure?" He nodded toward the couples gathering in formation.

I smiled and nodded. We joined the dancers, clasping hands with them. The music began.

"You've been avoiding me," the prince said near my ear when the dance steps brought him near.

His nearness caused me to miss a step, but he caught me. "On the contrary," I replied. "I'd hoped to speak to you much sooner."

The dance changed direction and we were pulled away from each other, weaving in and out with the other couples, then reuniting a few moments later. We joined at the elbows and spun.

"Ah, then I have kept *you* waiting," Henry grinned. "I must apologize. You seem quite serious. What would you speak to me of?"

"I owe you an apology," I said, trying to smile without my lips quivering.

The prince raised his brow. "For what offense?"

"My presumptions you had feelings for me. I behaved abominably that day you left."

His smile faded. "You were but a lass. I have changed too."

"I knew better." What did he mean he'd changed? Did he have feelings for me and now no longer did?

"You did, did you?" A glint flashed in his brown eyes. "Then I suppose I must consider whether I should forgive you or not. Perhaps I should consult with your parents on the matter?" He glanced at them.

Maman glared my way, *Père* watched us expectantly.

"Your mother appears to despise me as much as ever."

"I would certainly advise against speaking with them." I nervously laughed, considering the scolding I would get if my mother knew what we were talking about.

Our eyes locked for a moment before the dance required us to join hands with the others again.

Once reunited, Prince Henry said, "I must admit I was surprised to find you had accepted the invitation to come to court. Have you found it to be as sinister as you'd feared?"

"I believe sinister was the word *you* suggested." I smiled at him. "Happily, the demons I feared at court may yet prove to be phantoms of my imagination."

"I'm pleased to hear it," Henry replied. "I wish I felt the same. I'm afraid I've found King Stephen's court much less friendly than King Henry's. My demons are very real."

My eyes followed Prince Henry's to the king and queen seated at a banquet table—both watching us as intently as my own parents.

We moved across the floor to the music.

I nodded. "Perhaps you will need a champion to fight *your* demons." My reply came just as the dance ended.

The prince laughed. "And would you be that champion, Lady Ada?"

"I would fight for you," I answered before I could stop myself.

Henry smiled broadly, clearly amused at my candor.

Did he think I meant I'd fight for him as a mate? Heat rose to my cheeks. I curtsied and quickly walked away.

I took several steps toward my parents before the prince caught my arm, slowing me down.

As we approached my parents, one of the king's messengers tapped Prince Henry's shoulder. "The king requests your presence on the terrace."

Henry took both my hands and pressed them lightly before releasing me. He bowed to me and my parents, then followed the messenger through the crowded hall.

Rejoining my parents and Gundred, I was greeted by approving smiles from all but *Maman*.

"What happened?" she asked. "Why did you rush away from the prince after dancing?"

"*Oui*," Gundred chimed in. "What did he say to you? You look quite flushed."

"Nothing . . . of interest," I stammered.

"My child, you do not seem to grasp the importance of our presence here," *Père*'s voice was low. "You must understand the influence you would have, should the king choose you as Prince Henry's bride."

After all the years of trying to push away the memories of Henry, it was hard to believe marrying him could really happen.

"I do not agree with this," *Maman* said to my father. It was obvious they had already had this conversation.

My father ignored her and grasped my hand. "My Ada will do everything in her power to use her influence to maintain peace." He winked.

I suddenly recalled our conversation in the abbey. Was this what he'd referred to?

Only a few days ago, the mere suggestion of my becoming someone's bride would have stirred up a barrage of emotions from fear to anger, but tonight the idea ignited me. Why the change? Being in Henry's presence roused my nerves, but the actual idea of having power to change people's lives gave me a sense of fulfillment I had not considered—as if that were what I'd wanted all along, even though I hadn't realized it. I couldn't begin to understand the influence I might have over our two kingdoms, but I was not afraid. I wanted to learn.

"Ada, are you listening?" *Maman* asked sharply.

"*Oui, Maman*," I said calmly. "You needn't worry. I understand."

Almost a quarter of an hour passed, and Henry still hadn't reentered the hall.

"I'm beginning to wonder if he's coming back at all," *Maman* said. "I'm afraid I must retire."

"*Oui*," Gundred yawned. "I shall come with you."

Reluctant to follow *Maman* and Gundred, I glanced at the door, longing for just one more look at his face before bed.

"Might we stay for one more dance, *Père*?"

My father smiled at me tenderly. "Of course."

We joined several others on the floor. *Père* took his place in the inner circle, and I on the outer. Not a word was spoken, but my father wore the same expression I'd seen when we'd gone to the abbey together. I could feel the sentiment in his eyes. Perhaps he thought he'd soon be giving away his youngest daughter.

Before the dance finished, the door I'd been watching so carefully swung open. Prince Henry stormed back into the room, but he didn't stop to look for me as I had hoped. Instead, he pushed his way through the onlookers and made a hasty exit into the gallery.

I stumbled, but quickly regained my footing, and continued the dance. My heart felt as if it might burst from my chest. What had Henry's conversation with King Stephen been about?

Queen Matilda must have shared my burning curiosity, for she immediately excused herself and joined her husband on the terrace.

CHAPTER TWELVE

That night I dreamed of being introduced to illustrious royals from England, Scotland, and foreign countries. It was not the king and queen who stood in the reception line as hosts, but Henry and me. The long line of dignitaries reached a point I could not see, all presented to us one by one. I was not nervous, and Henry greeted each person warmly but with authority. He occasionally wrapped his arm around my waist and a deep happiness swept through my soul.

When I awoke in a strange bed, reality pierced my heart. My dream had only been fantasy. I hardly knew Henry's heart or he mine. We'd had all of one meaningful conversation these last few days. How could I expect to become his wife? There were more than a dozen others vying for the same. Thus far we'd only been friends. *Maman* was right—I needed to converse more with others and appear the noblewoman I was.

Maggie came into the chamber carrying a tray of food. "Are you awake enough to eat?" She set the tray by my bed. "Your parents are anxious to begin the day. I believe your father knows the prince's schedule today and wants you in every room he'll be in." She laughed at the idea.

I groaned. This was going to be harder than I imagined. I feared I'd appear as a candidate for auction, not a noblewoman at all.

That morning, I watched Prince Henry practice swordsmanship with my brother William. All the young women I'd seen from last night were there also, too elegantly dressed for such an event, as was I. In our overdone clothing of silks and velvets with headbands and belts of gold and silver, we were each directed to sit on the front bench, as if perched to be examined and bought. It reminded me of the time I saw Cook at the market considering a row of plump pheasants hung before him. He meticulously inspected their size, feet, beaks, and under each wing before choosing which bird he'd buy.

Prince Henry never looked my way. He didn't appear to notice any of the female onlookers, but I enjoyed watching him to my soul's content without him knowing. He was as tall as William but with broader shoulders. I couldn't stop staring at his strong jaw as he maneuvered and concentrated on the execution of each jab and swing.

At the noon repast Henry dined with the queen and the family of the black-haired beauty. Henry was in conversation with her constantly—laughing at what appeared to be her jests, then leaning in to speak of something more private.

My chest tightened. "*Maman*, do you know who sits with Henry?"

She clicked her tongue. "*Ma chérie*, that is Lady Cateline, the daughter of the Earl of Richmond. They have *Français* family ties."

Under my father's breath he added, "She may be your foremost competition."

Competition? A game to capture a prince. To get Henry, I had to play whether I wanted to or not.

After the meal we retired to our rooms and changed into something more suitable for games in the gardens. Later, as we strolled across the freshly cut grass, I placed my hand on *Père's* arm, all the while watching for Henry. Many of the young women and their families played quoits, tossing colorful rings toward a stake in the ground.

Reginald asked, "Can we join in?"

"I'd rather find where Prince Henry is before deciding what activity we'll undertake," *Père* answered.

I'd never thought my father could be such a matchmaker but him considering Henry as a husband for me was much better than some old nobleman I'd never met.

A jester in silky tight hose and a long, motley colored coat passed by on stilts, his fool's cap jingling with bells as he sung a high-pitched tune. "Here we go a-hunting for him who chooses a bride."

Reginald snickered.

I took a deep breath. This all felt unnatural and foolish, yet it was probably the most important game of my life.

We came around a tall beech hedge. I spotted Henry on a stone bench with Lady Marie, a young woman I had met and liked because of her ready smile and friendly conversation. They sat rather close in such a deep discussion that they didn't look up at our approach. For the second time that day my chest tightened with jealousy.

Henry obviously was singling out the women he preferred, then spending time with them to better decide the partner best suited for him.

I was not one of those favored. As if milk curdled in my stomach, I suddenly felt sick. Obviously, Henry hadn't forgotten our first meeting when I'd acted childish and rude. Or a few nights ago when I'd sat at the king's table with naught to say. I hadn't even greeted Henry appropriately. Those were not the actions of a future queen.

We walked past Henry. I tried to act as if the scene before me did not affect my emotions, but my legs stiffened into wood.

Père placed his hand over mine and squeezed. "If he does not see you as the fairest choice then he is a fool."

"*Merci, Père*," I said through a tight throat, wishing I were in my chamber so I could cry.

The next two days were much like the first, with Henry choosing other women with whom to spend his time.

It turned out there were more than the dozen young women from the swordsmanship display. Where they came from, I could not tell. I had no idea there were so many eligible daughters of nobility. Even daughters of French royalty walked the halls and gardens.

I thought again of Cook at market during the full bounty of harvest season where he could choose the most desirable fare. The crop being inspected here consisted of women with brown, blonde, and red hair, all dressed in their best finery and manners. Some held their heads in superiority, while others chose a more docile look of dignity. The lovely Lady Cateline appeared to be the favored choice of Prince Henry. I'd spied him strolling with her last evening after supper.

Not only did he not ask for my company again, but he also never looked my way. I once again felt destined to marry an old man not of my choosing. I was foolish to think my life was my own. I left the Great Hall with all its grandeur and headed toward the quiet and holy chapel. God alone could comfort me in the way I needed, as He had when our kingdom went to war with Scotland.

CHAPTER THIRTEEN

I didn't sleep well that night. Henry was in my dreams again, always just out of reach—in another room, behind a hedge in the garden, or surrounded by beautiful maidens. I was desperate to be near him. The unsettling feeling from the dream lingered in wakefulness.

"You don't look well this morning," *Maman* mentioned. "Are you ill?"

"I'm a little tired," I replied.

"Perhaps you should stay in your bedchamber and rest." She fiddled with her necklace. "I will have some bread brought up for you."

I shook my head. "I believe a bit of fresh air and exercise will do me good."

Maman agreed with a nod.

Père had been called to an advisory council with King Stephen along with the other nobles, so *Maman*, Gundred and I made our way downstairs and in the direction of the gardens. Before we reached the terrace, *Maman* and Gundred became entangled in a conversation with the aged Countess of Gloucester.

I rather thought I'd be trapped in the conversation as well, but *Maman* saw the despair in my eyes and made excuses for me not feeling well and needing air.

The fragrant smells of spring in full bloom refreshed and lifted my spirits almost as soon as I passed into the gardens. Though I'd only been away a week, my soul longed for the beauty and peace I felt at Reigate.

Removing myself as far as I could from the palace, I sat on a stone bench, nearly hidden from view behind a lilac bush. I couldn't resist soaking up the warmth of the sun on my face and arms. Convinced that my retreat was remote and undetectable—far from the usual paths wandered by the other courtiers—I pushed up my sleeves.

The bench sat against the outer wall of the palace and served as a suitable resting place for my back. Fully comfortable, I soon closed my eyes and imagined myself nestled against Beatrice's familiar trunk. Would she be surprised at my rapidly changing heart? How many times had she heard my complaints? Beatrice, more than anyone else, knew how I detested the thought of my future being chosen for me to suit the game of a king.

But when his game included Prince Henry, my resolution completely melted away, and all I could think about was the amused look Henry had given me when I'd stumbled over my words and promised to be his champion. It was very nearly the same look from so many years ago in response to my childish ramblings but magnified in intensity. Perhaps his look was magnified by the growing feelings . . . I had for him.

The amount of time I passed was unclear. If not fully asleep, my mind had drifted into the swirling realm of dreams when suddenly I was wrenched back to the world of Westminster Palace by the uncanny sense that someone was watching me.

Had I heard a twig snap? With consideration for the need to appear graceful and ladylike, I shook my sleeves back below my wrists, then turned my face toward the wall—as if it might hide my identity from the intruder.

"My Lady Ada, I didn't mean to disturb your rest." Prince Henry's voice both thrilled and panicked me.

I slowly turned to face him.

His expression bore the charming look of amusement I'd just been dreaming of. His brown eyes still reached into my heart and made it beat faster.

I rose and somehow found the poise to curtsy. "Your Royal Highness," I said in a calm, smooth voice that surprised even me.

"I must say that I'm very pleased to find you here. Had you been anyone else, it should have distressed me."

"Distressed, Your Highness?"

"Please," Henry took a step away from the path toward my sanctuary. "You must call me Henry."

"Henry," I said softly. It felt wonderful coming from my lips again and how I always thought of him anyway. But *Maman* would be furious if she were to hear.

He reached into the sleeve of his tunic and produced a small parcel wrapped in cloth. "Aye, distressed. Had you been another, I could not think of accomplishing the purpose for which I came to this very spot." He began to unwrap the bundle. "But as we are old friends, I do know we share a secret pleasure." Henry lifted the last bit of cloth. In his palm sat several small bits of amber sweetmeat.

"Honey sweetmeat?" He remembered us sharing the same treat at Reigate.

"Aye." He extended his hand in offering.

Without hesitation or thought, I reached for a piece and immediatcly put it into my mouth.

Henry smiled broadly, then took a piece himself.

"Delicious. It tastes exactly as the sweetmeats that Cook makes at Reigate," I said, hoping he'd remember. "Did you not say then they reminded you of your mother?"

He nodded and sat on the bench, handing me another piece. "She loved them and gave them generously to my sisters and me."

I reached for a small bit and slowly sat back down next to him. Once settled, I wondered if it was proper that I should be so near, but I didn't move away. "How are your sisters?"

"They fare well. Clarice married and has a child. Hodierne still lives at Scone."

He looked into my eyes, and I became aware of just how closely we sat. A thrill passed through me.

"You know, I believe you would find the grounds at Scone have quite a similar feel to your home at Reigate." As Henry described his connection to his family and home, it was almost like hearing my own voice. He talked of his childhood and the places he and Clarice had gone to hide away from life inside the castle. They even had a favorite tree, though when I asked him if they had given it a name, he laughed without answering. It became clear we had far more in common than just honey sweetmeats.

"I spent much of my time on the banks of the river Tay," he said. "As a matter of fact, that is why you found me near your pond the day we first met. I felt compelled to stop because that spot gave me such a sensation of being back home."

Learning these details brought both a mix of pleasure and empathy. He obviously felt homesick. I wanted to help him feel better but didn't know how. I sighed. "Cherchefelle seems to me the most magical place on Earth. And I can't imagine any other home than my dear Reigate. I'm sorry it's been a long time since you've enjoyed your home."

Henry's brows came together. "I've pondered on it and found that it's not my childhood home I miss as much as 'tis the people. They made it significant. Scone seems nearly lifeless to me without my mother."

My chest ached as I considered for the first time how Reigate would feel without my mother. If Reigate were a body, *Maman* was its beating heart. "I'm sorry," I whispered.

Henry went on to describe the changes that had taken place in his family since last we talked. His sisters had retreated from almost all public activity. He then spoke of his father still sorrowed after losing his mother. "His disposition became withdrawn. 'Twas almost like my mother's death snuffed out the last ember in the fire of his soul. I didn't recognize how much she'd safeguarded his heart until she was gone." He was silent for a moment.

"Your description convinces me that she was an exceptionally good woman." I wanted to take his hand, comfort him as well I could. But I could not, I should not.

Henry nodded. "She most certainly was. My father has been fortunate to be surrounded by benevolent, wise women since his birth. My grandmother was an angelic woman."

"I've heard tell of Queen Margaret's great kindness." I lowered my eyes. "The queens of Scotland leave very big crowns to fill."

The prince lightly lifted my chin. "Your spirit reminds me of them. They would have liked you."

The warmth evoked by his words and his touch filled my entire being. I could think of nothing to say in return. Lost in the depth of his brown eyes, I wanted to kiss him. I suddenly jerked back, embarrassed at how I'd let my thoughts roam. "My mother will be missing me by now," I said hoarsely.

His hand dropped. "Aye. You must go to her." He slowly rose from the bench. "Perhaps I will find you here again someday soon, my lady."

Was it a question or an entreaty?

"I will try." I curtsied and rushed away.

I felt Henry's eyes follow me down the path.

I found *Maman* and Gundred seated at a table on the terrace, not far from where I'd left them, still engaged in conversation with the countess. *Maman* held the woman's hand, listening kindly to her stories.

Gundred smiled when she saw me as if I were to be her savior. "Ah, Ada!" she called. "You look much improved. I believe the fresh air delivered just the medicine needed."

I blushed, wishing I could share with my sister the real remedy that had cured my melancholy. Sliding onto the seat next to her, I silently took her hand as I had many times when we were girls.

She smiled quizzically.

We sat listening to the countess's ramblings for only a few moments before the bellman announced the return of the king and his earls.

A group of bishops and other holy men in their church robes followed the king onto the terrace.

Père came directly to *Maman's* side and kissed her cheek.

The courtiers who had been wandering the gardens began to gather.

After a few minutes, Henry came from around the hedges. He nodded toward me and smiled, then found a seat easily within my line of sight.

"Lords and ladies!" The king's booming voice rang over the chatter of the company.

A hush fell.

"I hope you've been enjoying the beauty and bounty of my court. As your king, I am pleased to announce that we have reached a historic agreement with the Church. Together, we will work to reform the abuses of power perpetrated by former rulers. Some birthright lands will be restored."

The company cheered.

"In celebration of this new charter, I have a gift for you all. In a few days we will adjourn to Smithfield. My knights are prepared to entertain us with a show of their bravery."

I joined the company in cheering the king's knights, including William, whose skills had not yet been bested. My heart swelled with pride. I was finally to witness the pageantry of the joust.

The king's court was quickly proving to be the opposite of my expectations.

CHAPTER FOURTEEN

I flopped back on the bed. "You're a fool, Ada," I said to no one but myself. I regretted having left Henry so suddenly when sharing our time on the bench. I had wanted to kiss him and it unnerved me.

I worried at the inside of my cheek, chewing until I feared it would bleed. What if I came across as uncaring and my actions were enough for him to not consider me as a bride? He may think I am not intimate enough. I wagered Lady Cateline wouldn't have run off like a child.

I put my hand to my chin where Henry had held it. His touch had unsettled me.

Well, I needed to correct my error and show him I can be romantic. Can't I? I've never been before. How about captivating? "Probably not," I sputtered. What about seductive? I laughed out loud at that thought.

He'd told me often at Reigate that he preferred it when I spoke my mind. That didn't sound flattering, to be honest. But it did work well when all I wanted was his friendship. And didn't I still want his friendship? "It's decided then. Next time I have an opportunity to be with Henry, I'll bluntly tell him I'd like to be considered as his wife. But how will I get him alone again?" I'll have to visit the bench each day in hopes of spying him there.

Maggie opened the door and looked about as she stepped in. "Who are you talking to in here?"

"Just myself." I rolled onto my belly, my forearms propping up my chin. "How does one capture a man's heart?"

She laughed. "You'd best ask your sister. It appears she's married the man she loves."

Love. An array of emotions I never considered could be an element of *my* marriage.

I pushed myself to stand and Maggie smoothed my coral-colored tunic then clasped a gold chain to my waist, the ends sparkling with cut garnets. She brushed out my long hair and wove light green ribbons into one thick braid down my back and placed a gold band on my forehead and others on my wrists, then stepped away to examine her work. "You are lovely, Lady Ada. You've grown into a fine woman." She considered me a moment longer. "And if I may say one thing . . . I believe your duty to kingdom has kept you from having a childhood." She tapped her finger against her lips in thought. "It has kept you from examining and displaying what is truly in your heart."

"I was never allowed to display it."

"Exactly." She blinked rapidly and bit her lip. "I hope I have not overstepped with my words."

I looked away from her nervousness. "You haven't." She was right. I had kept myself from examining what my heart had been trying to tell me.

I wanted time to consider her words and stepped from the room. Although I needed to talk with Gundy, I suspected I should be alone first to organize my thoughts. As I strolled the hallways of the busy grand palace, I reflected on experiences with Henry and how I may not have understood my emotions.

I looked up to the magnificent fortress of stone and power as I walked. Its towering buttresses, imposing archways, and vivid tapestries that depicted valiant knights and scenes from battles won, all proclaimed the might of the English crown.

In the past, I had vowed not to let my emotions rule me, for my duty to king and country should outweigh the desires of my heart. I believed the king to be a chosen vassal of God. My conscience would not let me turn my back on that belief. He was more powerful than my father when it came to decisions for my future.

But was not the pursuit of love a path worth exploring? Indeed, many nobles had followed that path. Is that what I needed to do? I wanted to fulfill my duty *and* have a marriage of love. The two had always been separate in my mind, the latter unattainable. But now I wondered if they could be one and the same. I proceeded to the chapel where I prayed for answers until weary, then went to find Gundred.

On my way to her chamber, Lady Marie came toward me with her ready smile. Other noble maidens followed close behind her. "You are heading the wrong way," she said kindly. Dressed in a lovely butter-colored tunic with lavender embroidered flowers throughout, the color brought out the blue of her eyes and gold in her hair.

"What do you mean?" I queried.

The group of girls passed us with backward glances. No one smiled, although I smiled and nodded to them.

"All the maidens have been asked to have a noon repast with the queen."

"My invitation must have come whilst I was in the chapel." I followed the young women to the Long Gallery, the queen's personal reception room, only an eighth the size of the Great Hall but still expansive with pillars along its perimeter and wall paintings depicting religious scenes. The murmur of hushed conversations filled the space with about twenty present, dressed in every shade.

Although Henry wasn't there, I found myself surrounded by noblewomen who would be vying for his affections, and it felt

97

surreal. My heart, irresolute as it was, trembled beneath the weight of uncertainty and longing to be chosen.

As I neared a pillar, I noticed a few women huddled close together, whispering.

Whispering meant secrets and my curiosity piqued. I stopped behind the thick column, trying to make out their words. I heard my own name mentioned and frustrated sighs followed.

"This repast is just a formality. I believe it's Lady Ada he'll choose," one of them whispered. "Her father is the wealthiest and she's terribly spoiled, just the type a prince will want."

I smoothed at my silk tunic with trembling hands. Did they really think so little of me? I vowed to be less reserved and make friends with more of them. Every woman here was of noble birth but that didn't mean they had wealth. I looked about and realized I *was* dressed finer. I wanted to run back to my chamber and change.

"Nae, I do not believe it." That was Lady Cateline's smooth voice. "She may dress better than us and wear enough gold to light up a room, but Prince Henry had held my hand and told me how beautiful I am. I think the king will choose me as the prince's bride."

Henry had held her hand. Was that more tender than touching my chin? I think it was. My stomach hardened in jealousy.

"Ladies," the royal bellman called out to us in the room. "Her Royal Majesty, Queen Matilda enters."

I stepped out from the pillar, behind the backs of the whispering women, who now faced a door where the queen was expected to arrive.

The bellman opened the door and the queen entered with a smile on her face. She was a beautiful woman with delicate features. She moved toward us with elegance, her gown a shimmering blue and silver. The white wimple over her head was held in place by a simple gold crown with four stylized *fleurs-de-lis* sprouting from the top rim. Two long, dark brown braids draped her shoulders and flowed past her waist in front of her.

In her early thirties and mother of four young children, I believed the queen to be of stronger character than her husband but would never voice such an opinion aloud. She supported the king in his struggle to hold onto the English throne against their mutual cousin Empress Matilda. Before becoming queen, she was the Countess of Boulogne. Her mother Mary was sister to King David of the Scots, which made her Henry's cousin.

We all greeted her with a deep curtsy, the heavy skirts of our gowns rustling like autumn leaves.

"Come join me at the table." She beckoned us forward. "I have arranged entertainment for our day without men." She smiled with a gleam in her eye. "I am hoping to become better acquainted with thee."

One long table was laden with delicacies that spoke of opulence. Roast meats glistened in juices, carrots, peas and onions covered in herbs, and platters of cheeses and exotic fruits. Goblets of fine wine sparkled like liquid rubies.

I self-consciously scanned all the women, wondering who was the highest in peerage and would sit to the right of the queen. Her niece was the one and, knowing her place, settled in her chair after the queen sat. The rest of us were uncertain who should sit where and sat in whatever seat was closest to where we stood. I was a few chairs removed from the queen.

I glanced at the other women around the table. Some looked as young as twelve while others in their early twenties. Lady Eleanor, with auburn hair and lively green eyes, was known for her sharp tongue. Lady Isabella, on the other hand, was a delicate beauty with golden curls and a penchant for poetry. And then there was Lady Beatrice, who had a regal air about her but also a very large nose. I couldn't imagine any of these women by Henry's side.

The conversation flowed like a twisting river, and I found myself engaging in trite banter with my fellow ladies. Lady Maribella, to my left side, spoke of courtly matters and secrets that danced on the edge of scandal, all the while laughing softly. I wasn't used to such conversations with only my brothers to visit with me at meals and in the evenings in the solar. Their talk was of jousting or horses or hunting, and the like. I said little back to Lady Maribella, but she didn't seem to notice, her stories trailing long.

When she finally stopped to nibble something, Lady Cecilia leaned in close to my right ear, her voice hushed. "Have you heard, dear Ada?" She waited and when I did not reply, she went on, "Prince Henry has been seen strolling in the gardens with Lady Eleanor more often than not."

I turned to face her more fully and realized she was one of the women whispering near the pillar. Was she trying to provoke me? I didn't trust her. "*I* have not been watching him so closely," I said rather ignobly. "I'm already his friend and will soon spend more time with him myself." Why did I say such a thing? What if my words traveled back to Henry? I swallowed and took a deep breath, humbling myself with a private reprimand. "I am sure he has enjoyed Lady Eleanor's attentions. He is a kind man and will treat all noble women with care." If any of my speech does find Henry's ears, I hoped it would be my kind words instead of ungenerous ones. I tried to hide a pang of jealousy as I pictured Henry with Eleanor. "Lady Eleanor and the prince must be forming an amiable connection." I feigned nonchalance but realized I was rambling now.

Lady Cecilia nodded, then turned toward her other neighbor and spoke quietly with her.

I was not a bad person, yet these women seemed to bring out the worst in me. I needed to apply the manners I'd been taught all my life and not let my emotions rule my speech. If I were ever to be a leader, I would be required to be more diplomatic like our queen. I glanced at her at the end of the table.

She met my eyes and smiled genuinely.

I allowed a grin and bowed my head, hoping she realized I felt only benevolence for her.

Toward the end of the meal, she extended her hand to us all. "My husband's announcement that an English wife for Prince Henry would help us become stronger allies with Scotland was correct, but I want you all to know if you are chosen, the honor will be upon you as a loyal citizen to our country. The king will not make his decision lightly and has asked me to interview each of you tomorrow."

Lady Eleanor and Lady Isabella exchanged contemptible glances, their rivalry simmering beneath polite facades. I felt a knot of unease in the pit of my stomach.

Soon after, the jesters and minstrels entertained us with tales of chivalry and heroism, and female laughter echoed through the hall. I looked about the gathering of noblewomen, all vying for the same prize—the hand of Prince Henry—and I couldn't help but feel the weight of expectation. After all, he would take an English bride before the spring's end if the king was to be believed.

CHAPTER FIFTEEN

With a servant guiding the way, I walked along the edge of the lush green cloister lawn, a stone balcony above casting shadows around its rectangular perimeter. Herbs and late spring blooms lined the path to Queen Matilda's state chamber, their fresh fragrance potent.

I smoothed the folds of my deep emerald gown, adorned with intricate golden embroidery that shimmered with every step—a gift from *Père*, who didn't spare expense, hoping to ensure me the most resplendent among the English court. The whispering noblewomen yesterday had been right about that. But today, my attire wasn't just for my own vanity; it was a symbol of my father's ambition to secure our place at the heart of power. He told me this morning I could be just as important as my brothers when it came to our family's political influence. I was surprised at his honesty, and after having a long conversation about what I should say to the queen, I realized he didn't become the man he was without those beliefs.

Clothing could mean power in this game I played. What else did a woman have to show her potential? My education took second seat to my appearance. A shame, but the way of court pretensions.

Père had explained the importance of this marriage between an English maiden and the Scottish prince. King Stephen needed more allies—the whole kingdom of Scotland if he could—to make his realm that much stronger against the usurper, Empress Matilda and her son, who felt the kingdom legally theirs.

I couldn't help but feel a flutter of excitement as I approached the open door, where Queen Matilda awaited. Though eager to please her, the task at hand weighed heavily. The fate of Scotland's queen may rest in our conversation today. A marriage between Prince Henry and myself was not a matter to be taken lightly by the leaders of my country. I took some deep breaths and flexed my fingers, trying to repose myself.

The servant ushered me through the door with a sweep of his arm and I found myself in a kind of waiting room with no windows and settles against every wall. Torches lit its interior, even during this bright day. Lady Cateline paced across the room, and ladies-in-waiting lounged along its perimeter.

"Good day," I greeted them all. "Lady Cateline," I inclined my head when she turned at the sound of my voice. Her face was easy to read, and I was surprised at the disdain I found there when she didn't even know my true self.

"Lady Ada," she replied.

I decided to get the upper hand with my kindness and said, "You are lovely this day. May your interview go well with the queen."

She lifted a brow. "And yours," her words dragged indelicately.

She was short on conversation, and I decided not to push it further. I sat amongst the other ladies and visited about Reigate and their own homes.

Lady Marie came out of the queen's chamber with an unusually solemn expression considering she was typically the happiest among us.

I smiled at her, and her own smile appeared, but her eyes remained worried.

Cateline was shown into where the queen resided by a lady-in-waiting.

I stood and stopped Marie before she left the room. "Was it really so bad?" I whispered.

"Be prepared to share your heart for I believe the queen can see it. She is wise and gave sage advice, but I fear she does not see me as Prince Henry's bride." She looked at her clasped hands.

I could not tell her I was sorry to hear that because I was overjoyed. It was Lady Marie's goodness and her sweetness that I worried would attract Henry. I guessed there was more to a queen than kindness but what those attributes were, I wasn't sure. "I fear I'll fail in the queen's eyes also."

"Good fortune to you then." She smiled sadly and left.

After some time, Lady Cateline emerged, her head high but eyes averted from me. She swiftly left the room, her footfalls clacking away. She did not appear discouraged as Lady Marie had.

One of the ladies-in-waiting stood and motioned me forward. My heart hitched up a beat or two.

Entering the queen's chamber lit by tall, arched windows and candles throughout, I curtsied gracefully and the door behind me clicked closed to leave me alone with the queen. I had no doubt the room was designed to intimidate and impress. The sideboards were gilded in gold and candelabras glimmered with gold as well. The ceiling was an intricate working of beehive shapes and painted in blues and reds; the walls paneled and deeply carved with religious scenes. But I had no time to gape for the queen awaited me.

She sat high upon a stone bench, above three broad stairs, her gown a tapestry of rich blues and purples. Her eyes commanding but honest, she held an air of authority that was both awe-inspiring and terrifying. "Welcome, Lady Ada."

I found myself admiring her once again. "Your Grace," I began, my voice too quiet and tinged with nervousness, "I am deeply honored to be in your presence today."

She offered a warm smile as she motioned me to come closer. "The pleasure is mine. Your reputation precedes you as a charming and clever young woman." Her voice held a soft, lilting tone, carrying the dignity of her station, but I wondered if she said those same words to each noblewoman who came for an interview.

"*Merci*, my queen." I bowed again.

"*S'il te plaît*, come sit by my side." She pointed to the stone step just below her.

My footfalls echoed the distance between us. I settled onto the ledge, feeling its coolness seep into my skin. Already trembling, I shivered imperceptibly and turned slightly sideways to better look at her, and wondered how long I could sit so uncomfortably without shifting. I pulled my shoulders back, determined to be gracious, ready to start the interrogation.

"I have many interviews to perform this day, so let's not waste our time and get to the point. Tell me, my dear, how do you find the notion of becoming the Princess of Scotland?"

She truly wasn't going to dither. My throat dry, I tightly swallowed. "It would be an alliance that benefits both our realm and Scotland's, Your Grace. King Stephen seeks to strengthen his hold on the throne, and a pact with Scotland could be a powerful alliance against Empress Matilda's ambitions."

She studied me. "Indeed. I'm sure you understand that you are not the only noblewoman vying for Prince Henry's hand. There are others who seek the same alliance, and they too have *their fathers' ambitions* at heart."

I groaned inwardly, acknowledging the fierce competition that lay ahead but also that she suspected my words were my father's. "I am aware, Your Grace, and I am prepared to prove *myself* worthy of such an honor."

"It seems the Warennes are flourishing." She did not smile or change her imposing stature.

I blushed. Was I an investment and my father's wealth a determining factor in choosing Henry's mate? Or did the decision made by my king and queen solely depend on the noblewoman being a companionable wife to Henry? Or did they only want to know I had leadership characteristics? My confusion made my toes curl in my shoes. "It is true. My father's endeavors have been fruitful," I answered with little fortitude.

"It will take more than finances to determine the Scots stay loyal to King Stephen, not Empress Matilda."

"I understand. But it doesn't hurt to have assets available if a battle ensues."

I thought I heard her sigh. Her shoulders relaxed a fraction. "Such things should be discussed betwixt the men." She sounded as if she were reprimanding me for my comment, as my own mother would.

I feared I was doing poorly with this interview.

"What makes you believe you should be Prince Henry's wife?" One eyebrow lifted in question.

"A queen must have bravery, grace, and insightfulness. People recognize her as a leader only if she stands by her king. I will do that and more. I will serve my husband and new country with God by my side. I will continue what the past queens of the Scot's have done and serve as a pious leader."

Queen Matilda's gaze softened, and she reached out to pat my shoulder. "I have heard tales of your outspokenness, Lady Ada. But remember, the heart must also play its part in a marriage. Prince Henry is a man who deserves a wife who can truly capture his affections."

My heart slowed to a pounding. "I shall do my best to win his heart," I replied, my tone carefully composed but my emotions crashing down with uncertainty. "This is the component I am not sure I can attain—Henry's heart."

The queen's chuckle rang soft and caring. "Ah, love, such a delightful and unpredictable thing." She leaned closer, her voice dropping to a conspiratorial whisper. "I believe I detect more than ambition with you. I suspect you already have feelings for my cousin. I have seen the way Prince Henry fondly looks at you, Lady Ada. And there is also a seriousness when he speaks of you."

My cheeks flushed with warmth, and I stammered, "I assure you . . . I am committed to this alliance for the sake of England and Scotland, not merely for my own desires." Saying the words made my chest swell. I truly wanted to serve. But I also wanted Henry.

The queen sat back, a shrewd look of seeing right through me as Lady Marie had voiced. "Of course, my dear. But remember, sometimes it is the genuine feelings of the heart that make our kingdom stronger."

"You will be my example in all things, Queen Matilda." For it was believed her marriage to King Stephen was one of love and that she would do all in her power to support him. "With you being born the granddaughter of the King of Scots, I suspect there is much you can teach me."

She gazed at me as if pleased by my words, a small smile playing on her lips.

A calmness came to me then and a clear hope for the future. All my life I'd been trained for this day, and I now understood the aspirations of my parents.

With this new clarity, as our conversation continued, the weight of my responsibilities settled upon my shoulders. I knew that I must navigate the treacherous waters of courtly politics with finesse and determination. My father's ambitions, the future of England and Scotland, and my own heart were all at stake.

We spoke at length about what *Maman* and I did for the poor and meeting the needs of others in Cherchefelle, and I also told her Maggie's story.

As I left Queen Matilda's presence, instead of nervousness, a knot of worry now twisted in my stomach. The other noblewomen competing for Prince Henry's affections were formidable opponents, and I couldn't help but fear that one of them might win his hand. I had to find a way to display my true feelings for him the next time we met, to ensure that our alliance would be sealed in love, not just in duty.

Each day I had been strolling past the stone bench in hopes of finding Henry there. After leaving the queen, I decided to do so again. The scent of blooming flowers hung heavy in the air, and the soft hum of bumblebees filled the silence as I walked farther away from courtiers enjoying games.

To my delight, I spotted Henry sitting on the hidden bench alone, looking toward the sky. As I observed him from a distance, I couldn't help but be captivated by his charisma. He would make a remarkable king.

A soft smile suddenly tugged at his lips although it appeared he looked at no one and nothing.

A flush of warmth spread across my cheeks. I wanted to be inside his head and know his dreams, for surely that's what he was doing.

What if I told him my feelings of love and he doesn't feel the same? What if my profession made our relationship awkward? "Be bold, Ada," I whispered to myself.

As I approached, he turned. "Ada! Lady Ada," he amended. He stood, extending his hand. "You look as lovely as the garden itself."

Although his words sounded trite, he appeared thrown off his usual demeanor. And his eyes took me in from head to toe as if he liked what he was seeing and wanted more.

I accepted his hand with a gracious nod and curtsy, relishing the touch of his hand. "Your compliments are always appreciated, my lord."

We sat and he did not release my hand.

"I come from a private audience with Queen Matilda."

Henry's happiness fell away, and he pulled his hand from mine. "I know of the interviews. It feels a bit embarrassing being bartered for. I fear my father would not like these proceedings and my advisor has sent him word of the happenings here."

"I understand the prospect of a strategic alliance. A marriage that would further strengthen the bond between our realms. But I must admit, I do not appreciate my future being decided upon by an interview either. Yet, I've known most of my life that I was to be a pawn for a king. Whether for Scotland or England or France, I fear these decisions are not my own."

"Nor mine." He leaned back, concern flickered in his gaze.

I nodded, fully aware of the weight of our circumstances. "Indeed, Henry. Their choice of your bride is of great significance, not just for your personal happiness, but for the future of our nations. King Stephen is steadfast in his determination to secure his throne, and an alliance with Scotland would fortify his position against Empress Matilda."

"I know it all too well." Henry let out a sigh, his expression reflecting the burden of his responsibilities. "I can only pray they don't make the decision in haste."

My heart ached at his response. What was it or who was it that he really wanted? I maintained my composure, determined not to let disappointment cloud our conversation. "I desire what is best for both our countries. I believe that a union between us could bring happiness, benefiting our realms as well."

For a fleeting moment, his eyes softened. "Us? Oh . . . aye, you meant *us* as in kingdoms." He looked away.

"Perhaps I should not have been so bold, but I meant *us* as in you and me." I held my breath, waiting for him to look at me again, my heart practically pounded out of my chest.

He did look and his expression was one of joy.

I let out a breath of relief.

He took my hand again. "You hold a special place in my thoughts. Your wit, your charm, your boldness, and I am learning you care tenderly for others, not just birds." He chuckled. "What are we to do if neither of us end up content?"

"Would it make you happy if I were chosen?" I pressed my lips together with a prayer in my heart that I wasn't forcing his hand.

He turned to me, a sudden flush on his face. "Let's walk."

He was stalling. Why? I stood and placed my hand on his arm, disappointed that we were leaving our private spot. I feared I wouldn't have the bravery to tell him the rest of my feelings if we had others who could see us.

We walked until a distant crowd would be able to make out who we were.

"I have long cherished our friendship," he said, his voice soft and intimate. "But there's a depth to my feelings that I've been hesitant to reveal."

My pulse quickened, and I wished I was looking into his eyes instead of at his profile. "Tell me, Henry," I whispered.

He leaned closer, his hand gently covering mine, his thumb caressing my wrist with a feather-light touch. "Ada, I think we are meant to be together." He turned, his gaze locking onto mine, unwavering and sincere.

For a moment, the world around us faded into insignificance. I didn't care who watched. A surge of joy and relief flooded through me, and I could no longer contain my emotions "I love you, Henry," I admitted, my voice filled with tenderness and passion.

A shadow of uncertainty filmed his eyes. He suddenly looked away and stopped walking, removing his hand.

I wasn't sure what had just happened, but I released my hold on his arm. "Did I say something wrong?"

He ran his hand through his hair. "Nae. Aye. I don't know."

"What's happening, Henry?"

Not raising his eyes to mine, he stepped closer, his hand gently cupping my cheek, his eyes on my lips. "You do not understand what 'twould mean to be my wife." He dropped his hand and looked away. "Just forget we had this conversation. You'll be better off not connected to me in any way." He spun and walked off at a hurried pace toward the group of courtiers.

My breath hitched and all coherent thought fled. Henry just told me he didn't want me as his wife.

CHAPTER SIXTEEN

Roger excused himself from his own chambers when he realized Gundred and my conversation had turned toward Henry's unforgiving rejection. "I'll just take the children for a walk," he said, slipping out the door.

With him gone, I could freely let my tears fall. "Gundy! I want to go home. There is no reason for me to be here now."

"Tell me his words exactly." She placed her hand over mine and squeezed. "Perchance you misunderstood him?"

"*Non*, I am sure not." I wiped my tears. "He said I'd be better off not connected to him in any way."

"That does sound a rejection." She frowned deeply. "But it also doesn't sound like Prince Henry. I think he would be more tender about a woman's feelings. I wonder if you could have misunderstood him?"

"I think not. He left me rather quickly afterward."

"What brought on the conversation of him telling you to not expect a connection?"

"I told him I'd had my interview with the queen, and he was not pleased. He said he felt bartered for and that his advisor was reporting to Henry's father this business of King Stephen finding the prince a wife."

"Oh dear! I had hoped King Stephen would have already approved his bridal intentions for the prince with King David. Roger had guessed not, for our king can jump on an idea and carry it through quickly before others have a say."

"Queen Matilda is Prince Henry's cousin and appears to approve of what her husband is doing."

"And Empress Matilda is a cousin to them all and is gathering an army against them. It proves that families can fight as if they had no familial relation at all."

"It is the way of power," I moaned, knowing full well I had so recently been willing to take sides and to accept such maneuverings by becoming Henry's wife.

"We are not here to solve those troubles, but to decide on what you should do." She smiled tenderly. "Do you love Prince Henry, Ada?"

Fresh tears washed my cheeks, and I couldn't speak for several minutes. "Aye. I told him so. How can I make this feeling go away?" I clutched at my heart. "The pain is unbearable."

"I do not have the answer to that. Could the queen have spoken to him before you and told him you were not to be considered?"

"I can't see how. I went directly from my interview to Henry . . . Prince Henry in the garden. She had someone waiting to be interviewed after me." I tilted my head back, willing my tears to stop. "Gundred, I spoke with Maggie yesterday and she told me I have avoided what's in my heart because of others' expectations . . . and since Henry has told me more than once that he appreciates it when I speak my mind, I'd decided to tell him my feelings."

"How did Prince Henry act before you told him you loved him?"

"Tenderly." I remembered his expression of joy when I'd told him I believed our union would bring happiness. "He actually told me he thought we were meant to be together. Why would he say that and then tell me moments later that I would be better off without him?"

"I cannot be sure, and I don't want to get your hopes up, but I suspect Henry is fighting his feelings for you. Why he would do such a thing, I am not sure."

Would Henry play with my expressed feelings in such a way? Anger flooded my body until it reached my heart. "I will not believe that he cares and again have my feelings of love thrown back in my face. I want to go home, Gundy," I all but yelled.

A double knock sounded at the door, and it opened. *Père* and *Maman* stepped in.

"Ada, your voice can be heard down the hall. How could you act so indecorously?" *Maman* clenched her hands and landed them on her hips.

My mouth clamped shut and I looked away.

"Forgive her *Maman*, she has had a retched experience." Sweet Gundred made my excuses.

"Did the interview go badly?" *Père* asked.

I shrugged. "I am not sure. The queen was kind but perchance I spoke too boldly in my beliefs?"

"She is a wise queen, and I would expect your boldness would interest her, not the opposite."

Maman made a noise like she wasn't sure about *Père's* statement. "I am relieved if this nonsense about you marrying Prince Henry is at an end."

Her words caused more tears. How long must I cry? Will this heartache ever cease?

Gundred gently explained my conversation with Prince Henry to my parents.

Père sighed and knelt beside me, taking my hand in his. "Perhaps your *maman* is right and it's for the best. We are not leaving. Instead, I will begin to look for another husband amongst the nobles who are here. I have let my hopes for Prince Henry go on too long. With the king's approval, perchance we can settle this once and for all."

Père's words 'once and for all' played in my head throughout the night. Although I hadn't slept well, in the morning I was resolved in my decision to approach Henry one more time and ask him to be clear with his intentions. I needed to know 'once and for all' if I had understood him correctly. I knew I could be asking for more pain, but how could my heart hurt any worse?

Regardless, I'd never been in love before. I'd never had the attentions of a young man. Had he wooed me with his handsome face, strong stature, and his intelligence? I hoped to be more open to the possibility that I had been mistaken in my feelings because of my *naiveté*.

Westminster Palace was huge, and I looked in every room I was allowed to enter. I strolled the gardens and watched groups play their outdoor games, but I couldn't find him. I walked slowly toward the hidden stone bench hoping he wasn't there. The place now held a bitter memory for me.

When I came around the tall bush, I found Henry. Not only him but Lady Marie too. They sat close and were in a quiet conversation, Marie's hand on his shoulder. Henry appeared to be contemplating whatever Marie said and had brought down his eyebrows and mouth. Dark smudges ringed his eyes. Marie had her usual pleasant and encouraging smile.

Although jealousy and anger caused my breath to come courser, faster, how could I deny that Marie would be the best choice for Henry? If I were to choose a bride for him, it would be her. Pain moved into my jaw from clenching my teeth and I backed away, leaving before they discovered my presence.

CHAPTER SEVENTEEN

The next evening, I attended supper and a dance in the Great Hall. It was to be the beginning of the celebration that would continue on the morrow when the knights would joust and show their prowess, competing for honor. Although I had begged my parents to not make me attend, they refused to comply and *Père* said it would be the best chance to see all the peerage at once and discuss who he'd like to consider for my husband.

The Great Hall was overly congested with the kingdom's peerage, all guests in attendance at once. Perhaps they guessed, as had I, that court events were coming to an end considering the queen had completed her interviews.

The doors leading to the courtyard and gardens were all open, capturing what air possible on a warm spring's eve.

I could feel Henry's eyes on me from where he sat on the dais to the right of the king. The queen kept bending around the king to speak with Henry, but he seemed to not engage in much conversation, instead watching my father glance about and then talk to me. Did Henry guess *Père* looked for my future husband? Did he care?

My old thoughts and conditioning—my lack of allowing tender feelings, Maggie would say—came to me in full force, attacking my vulnerability and reminding me I was meant for an older man, someone whom I couldn't love. A union that would benefit the king only. I told myself I was better off without Henry in my life, as *Maman* had always believed. I tried to remain numb to all feelings.

Yet, the anger I couldn't quite contain pressed at my gut until I couldn't eat. I pushed my plate away and reached for the horn of wine, filling my goblet.

Maman gave me a side-eye, but I did not care. Somehow, I needed to ease my pain.

After our meal, the minstrels livened their tune to include a rousing dance number. *Père* stood and asked me to join him in the next dance. Nearing the large group of those enjoying the frolic, he brought me close to a duke standing near the wall, someone *Père* considered would make a good marital match. He engaged him in conversation and the duke watched me closely as my father talked. His eyes held no vitality, lines creased his forehead, and his grey hair bushed out around his hat. He said something to *Père* about his wife dying in childbirth.

As if my ears were plugged, I could not follow their conversation. The noises in the huge room seemed muffled. When the music started up again, I was relieved to finally be away from the man with the tired eyes. I danced with *Père*, stumbling twice, and grateful when we finally sat again.

"May I have this next dance," someone said above me, and I thought my ears were still not working and looked to who made the request.

Henry reached for my hand.

I didn't want to touch him, yet decorum won when I glanced at *Maman's* sour expression. I placed my hand in his. An instant warmth ran up my arm and I willed anger to flood my body instead. I realized it worked when the anger reached my heart. *I will not be vulnerable again!* I could hardly place one foot in front of the other and my eyesight narrowed to only the back of Henry's tunic of blue as he pulled me along.

With the dance floor crowd, even tighter than when *Père* and I danced, we received many stares but neither of us talked to anyone. The music started and people jostled to join hands, but as I reached out to another, Henry pulled me away and quickly out the door, into the darkness of the garden.

"It appears you do not want to dance," I said through clenched teeth, trying to understand his motive. "I am weary from our last conversation and would like to go back inside." I pulled my hand, but he held tight.

He stopped near a lilac bush and turned to me, his chest just inches from my nose. "First let me apologize. I am a beast to have talked to you as I had yesterday."

I stepped back and refused to look at his face. Well past the torchlight from the Great Hall, a sliver of a moon kept us in darkness, out of the sight of others. "Why should I forgive you? And can't we just part without speaking, never to see each other again? It is what I prefer." I pulled against his hand again, but he wouldn't let go.

Laughter came from nearby.

Henry walked again, pulling me farther into darkness, past the rose garden. "I have much to confess," he said over his shoulder. "We cannot leave our acquaintance as it stands."

"But my eyes are again open to my future. My father hopes to find a husband for me soon."

He stopped again and drew me close.

I stepped away, wishing he'd acknowledge my last statement and let me go back to the celebrations. Need I push against him? I feared touching him, his body so near, causing a weakness in my legs.

"You must have done well with your interview with the queen. She has chosen you as my bride, but the king does not agree. He feels Lady Cateline's father has proven himself more loyal to him than your own. Your father supported King Henry and consequently he fears your father could easily be swayed by Empress Matilda."

"Everybody supported King Henry," I mumbled and rolled my eyes. "I don't care of political maneuvers. I'm sick of it all." I took a deep breath and added with indignation in my voice. "Do not marry Cateline."

"Why not?"

I peeked at his face and quickly glanced away. His eyes were too earnest and his presence too close. "I fear you would be miserable with a woman who is a backbiter and a shrew. She would not make a good wife or queen. Lady Marie is a much better choice."

"And why would you choose Marie for me?" he said keenly, as if we were talking about choosing which cheese would go with what wine.

"She is kind and the opposite of Cateline. You may think her docile, but don't let her quiet nature fool you. Her heart is good."

"'Twas only yesterday you said you loved me and today you're willing to give me away so easily to another?" He feigned laughter.

Which made me look at him again. He'd never feigned laughter around me before. I did not know this man. "Forget what I said. I am a fool. I'm sure you're more than willing to not . . . to not be connected to me in any way . . . as you remarked yesterday." Tears burned my eyes, and I swallowed quickly, trying to keep them at bay. My heart squeezed with the pain of remembered rejection.

"That is why I wanted to apologize. I did not mean what I said." He was speaking tenderly, restraining himself but leaning slightly toward me.

I suspected our nearness was affecting him as it was me. "Then why did you say it?" I wasn't going to let myself believe him so easily. I couldn't let him back in my heart. The pain of his dismissal still cloaked me in apathy.

"When you professed your love to me, I found myself wanting to tell you the same. That powerful emotion made me realize I cared enough to not want you hurt. I could not bear the thought of you being in danger because of me." He covered his eyes for a moment. "I'd had a meeting with my advisor just hours before I saw you at the bench. We spoke of my enemies and the threats to my life."

I suddenly felt dizzy and swayed.

He grabbed my upper arms.

"Your life is in danger?" The tears came this time, and I couldn't wipe them away because of his hold. I looked into his eyes and thought I saw longing, not fear. "Please tell me what you mean."

He pulled me into an embrace.

My sudden concern for him broke all the anger and apathy and pain. I wrapped my arms around his waist as if it were a natural thing and I needed to keep him there always. My love burned stronger than it had the day before.

He kissed the top of my head. "I love you enough to know that if anything happened to you, 'twould tear at my soul."

I looked up. The sudden touch of his lips on mine blazed through my body, spreading warmth into my veins until I relaxed in surrender as he added pressure to his kiss. I knew in that instant I loved Henry enough to fight for him to be my husband. How it would crush my world if I could not be with him forever.

We came apart and he brushed at my tears, a sad smile on his face. "I'm an idiot for not having realized how I could hurt you with my words. I am so sorry, but now what should we do?"

I kissed him once more, a quick kiss of undeniable hope. "Is it not obvious? We must find a way to convince the king to allow our marriage. The queen is on our side. That certainly amounts to something."

"But how do I protect you from the dangers of my station?" He nuzzled my neck.

I had to push him away so I could think. "Make me aware of the dangers, I suppose. Let the choice be mine of whether I can endure such things."

He pulled in a deep breath. "I am not surprised at your bravery, but you must understand there will always be danger in our lives." He looked into my eyes again and brushed his knuckles across my cheek, the trail of his touch a magical sensation. "There are those who seek to take the Scottish crown and scheme away the earldoms that are a part of it. Any descendant of previous kings of Scots—which are many—could be our enemies." Henry looked at me solemnly. "Perhaps our greatest threat lies with the people here in the Great Hall."

My eyes grew round and my mouth fell open. "How can that be?"

He held me close and spoke quietly into my ear. "Empress Matilda is in talks with my father about the northern lands he desires. If he will support her cause, such a commitment to her will bring the English crown against Scotland. I'm committed to honoring my father's decisions and to preserve the throne for my posterity. I will fight for it if I must. These threats and more will become your cross to bear as well, my dear Ada. Are you sure you want to take that on?"

"Are you saying you—Scotland—will again go to war against England?" I whispered.

"'Tis too early to say with finality what is going to happen. I am telling you the possibilities that are looming. If we marry, it should be soon, and we will head north immediately. But . . ." He pulled me into a tighter embrace. "We need my father's approval, not just King Stephen's. As I mentioned, a message has gone to my father to tell him what happens here regarding King Stephen finding me an English bride. It puts our treaty on shaky grounds. My advisor does not think King David will approve. My father is my sovereign, not King Stephen."

I burrowed my face into Henry's wide chest and pulled in his scent of cloves and citrus. "At last we are on equal ground and understand our desire for one another, yet we are still pawns to

120

the kings, waiting for them to decide our happiness. I will speak to them myself."

"My sweet, Ada. How I love you and your boldness. *We* will do what *we* can to convince both kings that we should wed."

CHAPTER EIGHTEEN

The next morning *Maman* stayed in bed, complaining of a headache, and *Père* decided to stay with her.

"The truth is"—Gundred informed me when we were alone with our servants attending to our *toilette*—"*Maman* never could stand to watch a jousting tournament. Even before William was a competitor."

"Have you been to one?" I asked.

"*Oui*," she whispered. "It's all very exciting. But I can understand how she feels, especially when I imagine my Roger atop a horse, wielding a lance."

It was nice to finally be old enough to watch my brother joust, but I was equally excited at the prospect of seeing Henry again. Every time I closed my eyes, our conversation and especially our kisses replayed in my mind. I had every hope that he'd seek out my company.

Looking at myself in the glass, I was pleased with the servant's handiwork. My cream colored narrow *bliaut* caused the dress to hug my body and accentuate my waist. Gold ribbon covered my hem, matching the ribbon woven into my braids. I looked very much the illustrious lady. *Maman* would be satisfied. And I hoped

Henry would be pleased. But I especially needed the king to see me as a future queen.

We found our cart waiting outside the palace with Reginald already inside, excited to see his brother joust.

Great billowing clouds filled the sky. The warm air had a feel of dampness. I hoped the weather would stay fair. My dress would not do well in the rain.

I searched the faces of the nobles in line to be transported to the tournament but didn't see Henry. Perhaps he had already departed.

Reginald couldn't stop talking about the tournament as we traveled, causing my excitement to also build as we made our way north through London and finally east just outside the city walls. As we traveled, I filled Gundred in on my conversation with Henry the night before.

"No wonder you have the glow of good health, and your smile is radiant," she said with a squeeze to my shoulders.

When we arrived at the jousting grounds in Smithfield, Reginald joined his friends and Gundred and I followed a procession toward the royal dais, constructed high for viewing the tournament. We were seated near the king and queen, just outside their collection of royal attendants, and close to center stage. Disturbingly, Cateline sat to the right of the queen. She smiled sweetly at me, and my gut told me her place of seating wasn't an accident.

Disappointment clouded my mood and not seeing Henry anywhere made it worse. Perhaps he would arrive late? But as time passed, the stands filled. I glanced back at the king and queen again to see if an empty chair awaited Henry's arrival. There was no vacant chair.

Gundred touched my sleeve, "I'm sure he'll be here."

"Is my anxiety so apparent?"

She took my hand and patted it gently. "You're restless and appear lost in thought."

I opened my mouth to tell her my concerns, but the blaring of trumpets interrupted.

The tournament had begun and the first set of contending knights approached the king's dais before lowering their visors. The gleaming armor, long lances, and horses cloaked in colorful noble family crests, enthralled me.

The crowd cheered, and hooves thundered. The lances crashed against armor, brutally knocking one of the knights from his mount.

Amazingly, he struggled to his feet.

High spirits built among the spectators as the knights rode each charge.

Finally, William rode out to compete, his horse draped in the Warenne checkered blue and gold. The top of his helmet bore a matching feathered plume. How could his heavy armor not be cumbersome? He moved like it were a linen tunic. One of the greatest knights in all of England and France, Gundy and I exuded with pride over his prowess and skills.

But it wasn't just skill. To be a knight one had to swear that he would defend the weak, poor, widowed, orphaned, and oppressed. He was to be courteous, brave, and loyal to the king, concerned about the welfare of his subordinates, or those of lesser rank and position. William represented all those things.

With William's first charge, he easily connected, leaving his opponent writhing on the ground. Making the sport look easy.

The crowd gasped.

When the man was unable to push himself up after several attempts, a team of the king's servants carried him off.

"Will he be all right?" I asked Gundred, feeling sick to my stomach. No wonder *Maman* stayed home.

"I do hope so." She shook her head. "He bled badly."

William braved two more courses with the lance, winning each match quickly.

After the third, King Stephen rose and walked to the edge of the dais, motioning for William to approach. "Sir William," he shouted, his voice silencing the crowd. "You have proven yourself the strongest of all knights. But before I declare you champion of this tournament, I believe we have one final contender."

A knight in highly polished silver armor with a red feather plume on top of his helmet charged out of the gate. His horse was flanked with gold caparisons with a depiction of a red lion on its hind legs.

The crowd cheered.

The knight pulled his horse to a halt in front of the king's stage and lifted his visor.

I wasn't prepared to see the warm, brown eyes of Henry. I gasped audibly, but the exclamation became swallowed by the roar of the crowd.

The king waved his arm to silence them. "Prince Henry of the Scots, your father has battled my armies in the North. We were prepared to defeat your countrymen at Durham before our treaty. You say you pay homage to me as your king and yet you refuse to accept the bride I've chosen for you. What say you, sir?"

My heart thudded against my ribs. The king had chosen a bride for Henry? He must have made a definite decision for Henry to wed Cateline. I glanced over at her, and she smiled smugly at me. Had her father already been told? Was all arranged?

Prince Henry nudged his horse closer to the stands. I detected the same fire in his expression that I'd witnessed on that first night at the banquet when he'd requested a private audience to discuss the matter of his marriage.

"I will gladly marry an English bride, but again I request that she be of my own choosing."

Was this how he was to gain our approval for marriage? I wanted him and it now felt so wonderful to know he wanted me. He was proving it here and now. But to leave our success to the chance of a joust? The decision to do so must have been his last hope. Or had someone else come up with this scheme? It reeked of King Stephen's doing. Henry didn't look at me or acknowledge my presence in any way. I *had* to suspect he had a strong plan.

"You'll find I'm a just and merciful king. And I'm inclined to grant your request." He laughed as if he enjoyed knowing something the rest of us did not. "But first you must learn that everything comes at a price." He motioned William to approach the stand.

William rode forward.

The king looked again at Henry. "Your fame is well known throughout Scotland." The king lifted his voice to the crowd even though his words were directed at Henry. "You are undefeated in jousting, are you not?"

"I am," Henry loudly replied.

"Then are you prepared to fight for what you want?"

Henry narrowed his eyes. "I am."

"This will prove to be a most exciting match." King Stephen looked above Henry's head at the crowd. "What say you? Shall we let the prince fight for his bride?"

The king stretched his arm toward Henry and the cheers were deafening. Then he stretched his arm toward William. Surprisingly, not many more cheered for him as for Henry. They appeared almost equally divided, perchance wanting to know who the prince would choose as a bride? Few people liked their decisions made for them. None would want to be a pawn.

I did not want either of them to lose, but there was much, much more at stake for Henry to lose.

I glanced sideways at Gundred, whose face had drained of color.

"Let the strongest win!" the king commanded, stomping back to his throne where Queen Matilda moved restlessly, apprehension pinching her face.

"And what say you, my queen? Your cousin wishes to disregard my council. He does not trust my wisdom."

The queen frowned. "I don't believe Prince Henry questions your wisdom, my lord. I fear he's simply lost his heart."

"And would you have me restore it to him?"

"It is within your power to do so." She raised an eyebrow and gave him a look of hope.

King Stephen brought his wife's hand to his lips. "Then so be it. Prince Henry may choose his own bride—provided he unseats Sir William."

She rolled her eyes, and I was convinced this competition was all the king's idea. He appeared to enjoy being an actor on a stage.

The crowd roared as the knights rode into place.

My heart pounded so hard I could feel it over the deafening clamor.

Gundred took my hand, squeezing a bit too tight.

The shouts and stomping rolled on and on.

The stage beneath my feet felt unstable.

Gundred clutched my arm to steady us.

I could barely comprehend what was to happen. In a matter of a few minutes, the king could twist my dream into disappointment. There could be no winner of this match for me. The honor and love of my family should be too great to *wish* for William's loss, yet I was doing exactly that.

William dug his heels into the flanks of his horse, thundering at a full gallop to the far end of the list.

Henry slammed his visor down with a clank. His horse reared back onto its hind legs, then bolted to the opposite end of the long run.

Queen Matilda gnawed on her lip, and I worried she knew something I didn't. "My lord, do you think it wise to insist on making Prince Henry win in order to choose his bride?"

King Stephen raised his hand sharply, silencing the queen. "I'll have none in my court or on the field of battle but those who have proven loyal to the crown."

The queen's glance darted between the king and her cousin. She clearly wished to help Henry, but to do so in such a public setting would almost certainly mean dishonoring her husband. We were all at King Stephen's mercy.

"On with it, then!" William's helmet muffled his shout.

For the first time, I considered William's wife, Adela. Had she come to watch him ride today? I looked right and left but did not see her. If I'd known Henry would be jousting, I probably would have stayed hidden under my covers at Westminster Palace with *Maman*. Poor Adela! How did a wife become used to sending her husband into danger? It must be so frightening every time men went off to war. I am asking for such a life by marrying Henry, yet I cannot restrain my love for the man.

"What can we do?" I whispered to Gundred.

"Pray," Gundred answered. "All we can do is pray."

I sent a heartfelt entreaty to God as both riders selected their lances.

The odds were on William. But was the competition fair since he'd already fought three jousts? Surely, he must be exhausted.

My stomach clenched, and I doubted I could ever eat again. *Please, God*, I begged, pinching my eyes closed and bowing my head. *Please protect them both. I cannot bear for either of them to lose.*

Before my eyes opened, the thud of hooves sounded against earth. My brother and Henry barreled toward each other at alarming speed. I watched through squinted eyes, my hands covering my mouth.

The riders brought down their lances.

Bracing myself for impact, I hugged Gundred close.

Both lances connected with the riders' shields in a great crash, pieces shattering from both.

The force of the blow threw William to the ground. He lay motionless as his horse continued to the end of the run.

Henry dangled precariously at the side of his horse; right foot caught in the stirrup. He slipped to the ground, seemingly unconscious, dragged several yards before he tumbled and rolled in the dirt.

After what seemed like hours, but was perhaps only moments, Henry revived and shoved himself to his feet.

I released my breath. To my great relief, he walked on steady feet. But all too soon, my worry shifted until William began to stir.

Within moments, he was on his feet, staggering toward his horse, ready for the next draw.

Three rounds were expected, and the crowd roared, anxious for the game to continue.

Gundred brought me into her arms. "All will be well. All *must* be well!"

The combat would continue with no slowing of pace, though both knights were wounded already. I began to think it might never end.

The second draw proved as the first. But this time, lances shattered against breastplates. Both William and Henry simultaneously flew off their horses. Henry now limped as he walked to his horse for the final and third round.

Anger bubbled in my chest for men who felt they needed to showcase their courage and skill. Such pride stymied my understanding. I kept replaying in my mind the lances shattering and imagined bones shattering too. I'd never fainted in my life, but I suddenly felt ill. "Gundy, I am not well."

She turned and said something to the queen's lady-in-waiting.

Black spots danced before my eyes.

Suddenly Gundred held a flask of distilled wine to my lips. "Here, drink some of this. Just a sip."

The smell alone made me awaken, jerking back in my seat. The alcohol burned down my throat but did revive me.

One of the ladies-in-waiting stood to my right, using a fan to create a breeze.

I gulped in air.

"Fare you well now, Ada?" Gundred's pinched and worried face came into better view.

"*Oui*." I gulped more air and took one more sip.

When I had my senses about me, I realized William and Henry were seated on their horses, waiting at opposite ends of the list.

Henry made the cross of our Savior, as did William.

Even with the attendant fanning me, sweat trickled down my back.

The trumpeter let out his blast, and the horses thundered forward.

"Please God, please, I beg Thee keep them safe," I whispered under my breath, my heart slamming against my ribs.

The crowd quieted.

Just as William's lance hit Henry's shield, Henry's horse rose on its hind legs. As if the world seemed to slow to a stop, Henry hit the ground.

"Henry!" I shouted, tears blurring my eyes.

William threw down his broken lance, still seated on his horse and turned toward the dais where the king had gotten to his feet. The crowd returned to life in a cacophony of shouts and cheering.

Henry stood slowly. His shoulders rolled forward, bending at the waist, he placed his hands on his knees. The stance of a man defeated.

Tears spilled down my cheeks and onto my tunic.

Gundred had stood, clapping for William, but I could not bring myself to do it.

William dismounted and waved to his supporters. The crowd cheered and stomped, waving the flag of England.

Reginald broke from the crowd and raced to his brother, taking him in a one-arm embrace. When Reginald stepped back, William knelt before the king, head bowed.

My great sadness and worry kept me from hearing the king's proclamations. I watched as Henry mounted his horse and rode through the gate, disappearing from my view.

CHAPTER NINETEEN

My emotions stretched so tight I felt sure that any compassionate touch might break me.

The king withdrew, followed by the queen and her attendants.

"We must see to William's wounds." Gundred took my hand.

I shook her off.

"Come, Ada, our brother may need us."

I nodded, but I was still in a daze as she led me through the crowd and past the field to the tents of the knights who had jousted.

When I was finally able to organize my thoughts, I asked her, "What will happen to Henry?"

"Hush," Gundred said. "*Père* will know what to do. Do not speak of it until we return to Westminster."

We found William with his squires. Attending to his injuries, they bound the gashes on his broad chest tightly in bandages while an apothecary announced broken ribs.

Gundred pushed her way toward William.

He lifted his arm to wave her over, then winced in pain. "I'm fine," he said before she could react. "You must make haste back to London. Adela will hear what happened and be worried.

Reassure her that I'll be back shortly." He was oblivious to what his tournament had meant to me.

My brother had been right. When Gundred and I arrived, Westminster Palace was buzzing with talk of the joust. Adela, *Maman* and *Père* had waited outside for our cart's arrival.

Gundred reassured them all that William's wounds were not life threatening. When we arrived at our chambers, she then with passionate accuracy recounted the details of what had transpired. She painted a scene of Henry fighting for my hand, which brought my emotions into sharper focus, and questions plagued my mind: Where was Henry? And what did his loss mean for us? Would Cateline be his wife?

Maman seemed to sense my distress and insisted I take some rest in my bedchamber.

"There is nothing for us to do now except to wait," she said, tucking me under the covers. It was kind of her to show me concern without speaking ill of Henry.

With tears once again near the surface, I closed my eyes. I knew I could not sleep, but I wanted to be alone.

Henry had defied the king's choice of a bride, I was sure of it. Would that go unpunished?

The next morning, *Maman* had the servants packing our trunks to prepare for our departure.

"But has Henry returned?" I asked in a panic. I desperately wanted to know if Prince Henry was safe and well. Did he have someone to tend to his wounds as William had?

Père nodded. "He is well and attended to, but there have been some changes. His advisor brought a letter from King David last night. He is disturbed with the way Prince Henry has been treated here. He demanded Henry return home immediately. Some are saying he's making his way back to Scotland even now. But others say he cannot leave because of the treaty between the two nations."

Something deep inside me feared the worst. King Stephen must be furious that King David has demanded Henry come home. Did this break the treaty? Or even worse, would we truly go to war with Scotland?

My heart hurt as if it had been pierced by a lance. "Send Maggie to me. I must dress quickly and find Henry."

I had no idea where Henry's chambers were or where to find him. The crowded halls filled with noble families departing and servants carrying trunks slowed me more than I would have liked. I wanted to run. But run where? I went to the Great Hall but for once it was quiet and empty but for servants cleaning. I cut through the lobby to the library but only found a few elderly gentlemen in there. I backtracked to the chapel and peeked in with no success. Where was I to find him? Every room open to me I checked. I feared I was wasting time when he may have already left. Giving up my search, I went back to my parents who told me the servants had left with our belongings and we were leaving immediately.

Coming outside to the palace yard, the air was a film of dust from so many carts having departed. The wide clearing bustled with activity, hostlers and servants going about their duties. The Warenne cart was among six still preparing to leave.

Robert and Waleran approached us to say their farewells.

"Ada!"

My heart leapt at the call, and I turned.

Henry exited a cart moving away, almost falling with the motion. He righted himself and ran toward me.

And I toward him.

He stopped just short of taking me in his arms for we had many onlookers. Out of breath, he grabbed my hands. "I've been searching for you everywhere."

"And I, you." I wanted to kiss him like we had the night before but felt dozens of eyes upon us.

"Forgive me," he said, his eyes moist with tears.

"For what?"

His expression registered surprise. "For not winning your hand in marriage."

"I would never blame you for that. I love you, Henry. What are we to do?"

"I've been called home, which breaks our treaty with King Stephen. My father is furious at the way I've been treated here, and as expected, he's upset at the king assuming the right to find me an English bride." He smiled softly, even with moisture in his eyes, and then touched my face. "My father doesn't know I've chosen a bride for myself. I will speak to him as soon as I'm able." A tear fell and he roughly brushed it away then took my hand again. "Ada, this problem is bigger than you and me. Our countries will likely go to battle again." He made a sound of great frustration.

I feared he'd cry more and wanted to be the strong one but couldn't find the words to comfort him because his loss was also mine. My heart felt as if it were in a vice.

"Not only is it likely we won't wed, but we may never see each other again." Another tear leaked out and he growled as he swiped at it.

"Oh, Henry! This cannot be. We must find a way." Hot tears broke free from me too. My throat constricted with the weight of unspoken emotions.

He pulled me into his arms so suddenly and with such force that I almost lost my breath. "I love you, dear one. You have given me so much more to live for—driven away my loneliness. I will do all I can to come for you. Don't give up hope and I won't either."

I grasped to him with such fear of never having this man beside me again. "I will pray daily for our union. God is good. He will help."

"He's all we can depend on, I fear."

"Remember when you once told me He gave you comfort at times of loneliness? I know he will do that again. Pray for me too,

Henry. Pray that I may have the same comfort for I will be lonelier than I've ever been in my life."

He pushed away slowly, looking as downcast as if someone had just died. His eyes looked at mine and I sensed desire. He laced his finger in my hair at the base of my neck, pulling me toward him.

Our lips met in a kiss like I've never received before, igniting a blaze of longing within me. I relished the pressure of his mouth on mine, willing to never forget.

He moaned and pulled away, placing his forehead against mine. "We've given everyone something to talk about. If we are lucky, it will reach the ears of my father."

A surge of desperation welled up inside me. "It must," I replied, my voice steady despite the turmoil in my heart. "Tell your father he will not be sorry if he chooses me. I have been trained all my life for this, Henry. Tell him that, and that I will serve your country with love and willingness, as I will also serve you."

Henry leaned in, his lips brushing against mine in a gentle kiss, a bittersweet promise. "I will say all those things and more. I will come back for you, Ada," he whispered, his breath warm against my skin. "I swear it."

"I will hold you to that promise, my love."

Though we found Reigate alive with spring's late full bloom, the mood of the household was somber. The servants spoke in hushed whispers, I assumed to aid William in his recovery. But I soon became aware that their compassionate glances were for me.

Père wasn't as sure as me that Henry could talk his father into letting him marry an English bride—a daughter of someone loyal to King Stephen. He started to consider other matches for me again, saying one would be chosen for me shortly. I pulled inside myself with no will to communicate with anyone.

135

By September, word came from a messenger that the treaty with Scotland had been broken and King David's troops attacked in the North with exceptional brutality.

"The Scottish knights are killing everyone in their path—men, women, and children," the messenger said breathlessly.

"Barbarians!" William huffed.

"They don't even spare the clergymen," the messenger added.

The news sent my mind reeling. I tried not to imagine my Henry and his involvement in such battles. Surely these were merely stories. He would never stand for such cruelty.

"Can we offer you some refreshment?" *Maman* asked.

The messenger accepted gratefully. The servants laid out our supper, and he joined us.

I could scarcely eat a bite. I listened intently to every word said, hoping to hear some clue about what was happening to Henry. Unfortunately, by the end of the meal, it became clear the messenger had already delivered the only real news he possessed.

When asked if he would stay the night, he declined. "I must return to London before dawn." The order was sent to the stables to have his horse prepared immediately.

William and Adela retired to their chamber.

As the messenger donned his cloak and placed his satchel over his shoulder, he startled. "Ah, aye." He reached inside the pouch. "I'd nearly forgotten." He turned toward me. "Lady Ada, I have something for you from the queen."

"For me?" My heart nearly stopped. When the messenger handed me a small brown parcel, my heart resumed, beating even harder.

Maman and *Père* both eyed me expectantly.

What could it be? The queen and I weren't acquainted enough for gifts. I slowly opened the small box.

Inside lay a bird, intricately carved from wood, delicate and painted with great detail. A sparrow. Sparrows represented hope. Could it be the queen was sending a message?

The gift came with no note of explanation.

My parents and the messenger looked puzzled, but my heart bubbled with expectation. Was it from Henry? He knew my love of birds. Was this a promise that he would return? Or was it the queen giving me hope that she could bring my happiness to fruition?

In May my strong and imposing *Père* suddenly fell ill with a breathing ailment. He was cared for in the very infirmary he'd worked so hard to establish. I could not bear to see him pale and feeble.

"Please, *Père*," I pled, kneeling beside him. "You must get well. I beg you, do not leave us."

Père's labored breathing paused, and he opened his eyes slightly. "Ada," he breathed. "Is that you?"

"*Oui, Père.*" I leaned closer. "I'm here."

"Fear not." He wheezed. "The . . . the queen. She is sympathetic. She will do all she can . . . to aid you."

I reached for his hand and held it tight. "What do you mean, *Père*?" It was a second witness that my hope should lie in her power.

Père closed his eyes again, his breathing rhythmic, and he did not answer.

I sat near him off and on for days, praying he heard my words of encouragement, despite his delirium. But he never reawakened. *Père* was badly outmatched by an invisible enemy that was quickly robbing his life from within.

His relatives who could travel came to join the bedside vigil. But regardless of our prayers and pleading, my father died. We buried him at his father's feet at the chapter house of Lewes Priory. My brother William became the 3rd Earl of Surrey.

My heart ached. I missed *Père's* love and strength and protection. He would have ensured that I was not given in marriage to someone he did not approve of or trust to care for me. But he was gone, and I was still a pawn—available for some nobleman to claim as the king saw fit. I would now be at my brother's mercy for the final decision. Would William be as particular as *Père* in his choice for me? I feared not as our relationship had been strained since the jousting match.

One day, in great mourning, I mounted Cooper and rode across *Père's* beloved land in solitude, looking toward an uncertain future. Had I the strength to handle the difficulties and challenges that awaited me? If knocked from my horse, would I find strength to rise again as Henry had?

Dismounting, I stood on the hill overlooking Cherchefelle. Loose tendrils of hair wrapped around me in the warm summer breeze.

I replayed in my mind for the thousandth time the jousting matches and how Henry had pushed himself to stand after being knocked off his horse so many times. If he could do that, couldn't I find strength in myself to take what was coming? *Oui!* I had the fortitude to press forward as *Père* would have me do—the fortitude to deal with whatever this life of nobility handed me. If not for myself, then for *Père's* honor and good name. And maybe for Henry.

CHAPTER TWENTY

Anno Domini 1138
Reigate, Surrey, England

"Maggie?" I called, peeking into the nursery. But I didn't see her, her boys, or Clare. They were nowhere in the castle's upper level.

Descending the stairs lit by morning sunshine, I found *Maman* in the hall, arranging flowers in a vase. "Where are Clare and Maggie?"

She tucked another stem into the arrangement. "I received word that Clare's mother is ill, so I sent her home to look in on her." She motioned toward the courtyard. "I think Maggie has taken the twins outdoors."

"*Merci, Maman.*" I turned to leave.

"Ada, might you be able to watch Maggie's boys for a short time this afternoon so she can get a bit of work done? Perhaps an hour? All the other servants have their duties."

"Certainly." I dearly loved them, though I still could not tell them apart. Turstin and Alric had grown to be so adorable at almost four years old. Maggie and I had spent many hours entertained by their whimsical little ways.

139

I hurried toward the door and found my boots outside under the eave. I pulled them on as voices and childish giggles came from the stable. Maggie must have taken the children to see the horses. It was one of their favorite pastimes.

When I reached the stable door, I stopped abruptly and stayed unseen.

Chadwick leaned against a pitchfork—tall and handsome with thick, sun-bleached hair—in a lively discussion with Maggie, who sat on a hay pile. Alric and Turstin wrestled beside her. Her eyes fixed on Chadwick, she laughed with delight, full of joy unlike I'd ever seen.

Turning, Chadwick saw me, and a blush rose on his cheeks. "Your horse will soon be ready, my lady." He went to the stall.

I hadn't come for my horse, but Chadwick's blundering made me feel embarrassed, as if I'd caught him doing something wrong. I did not call him back for correction.

Maggie stood and gave me an awkward formal curtsy. "'Tis a beautiful day for a ride. I hope you enjoy it." She took each of her boys by the hand and hurried out the door.

I called over my shoulder, "I will watch the boys later so you can help Clare."

After a few minutes, Chadwick appeared. "Here he is, my lady." He'd brushed Cooper to a glossy perfection. He handed me the reins. "Cooper is eager to get out to the fields today." He boosted me into the saddle.

I glanced back and watched Maggie enter the house. What had I just witnessed? I tried to shake off the feeling that Maggie and Chadwick kept a secret. Did they care for one another? A twinge of jealousy arose that they could choose their relationships, and I could not.

What must it feel like to love someone and have hope for a bright and anticipated future?

Maggie's weather prediction was right, the day perfect for a ride. The horse kept a steady, easy pace. I headed through the

140

rolling meadows, crossed the groves of trees in autumn colors, rounded the pond and deer park, all within the safety of Reigate land.

My mind wandered to life at home. What if Maggie were to marry and leave me? I'd come to depend not only on her help, but her friendship. The thought brought warm tears to my eyes that cooled on my cheeks as I rode. Even my friendships were not certain. I could not give my heart in love or affection without it being broken.

When I returned to the stable, Chadwick worked alone, mucking out a stall. The happiness he radiated confirmed my suspicions. Because he certainly couldn't be happy about mucking.

I should have been overjoyed, but sadness lingered as I entered the nursery and found the twins playing on the floor at Maggie's feet. I watched them for a few moments before lifting my eyes to Maggie. "*Maman* asked me to tend the children for an hour whilst you do housework."

Maggie nodded. Our eyes locked for a brief but uncomfortable moment. "I'm much obliged." She curtsied and hurried out the door.

In the following weeks, I refrained from asking her about Chadwick. I supposed she would speak of him when she was ready. I found myself more aware when she slipped from the house toward the stable. It happened more often than I'd expected— sometimes with a pastry in hand.

Adela had become mistress to Reigate when William became earl. That left *Maman* with less to do. She'd taken to visiting me early most mornings. Ofttimes, she'd slip into my bedchamber, and we'd speak of trivial matters; advice on my attire, news of the family, humorous blunders made by visitors. They were but commonplace exchanges, peppered with laughter and embraces—something I badly needed. But nothing took the deep ache away of losing Henry. The promises we made at parting seemed unattainable as the war with Scottland continued. To William, Henry was the enemy.

Gundred sent me missives, surprised William had not approved a husband yet. I was certainly old enough to play my part for the king. I didn't know how to answer her. Perchance William was too overwhelmed with his new responsibilities to worry about me. I certainly wasn't going to encourage a match.

I blamed my melancholy on autumn, for Reigate's trees were dropping leaves that carpeted the forest floor. The days had become chilly. Nights were spent lonely by a fire in my room. My thoughts often crept back to the gardens at Westminster last spring, and I longed for just one more afternoon in the sunshine, sharing honey sweetmeats with Henry. Or a passionate kiss in the dark. I wondered what he was doing now while the fighting in the North continued. Did he ever think of me?

One afternoon while standing at my bedchamber window, I saw Maggie leaving the stable, almost skipping. That familiar twinge of envy grew within me. I wanted to be happy for her, so why did my heart covet her joy?

I looked deep for the answer. Pawns rarely had the chance to marry for love. I had almost been given that chance, but my happiness had been snatched away.

"Lady Ada, I need to speak with you." Maggie said from behind me.

Startled at her assertiveness, I turned to find her standing in the doorway.

She stepped into the room. "I need to tell you that . . . well, I'm getting married." An excited smile played upon her lips, yet she lowered her eyes to the floor as though her happiness would somehow hurt me.

And it did. But I tried to hide the ache in my chest. "To Chadwick?"

"Aye." She looked up. "Since you saw us in the stable that day with the twins and had said nothing to me about it, I worried that you were angry." She clasped her hands as if in prayer. "I ask of you, please do not be. Let nothing come betwixt us."

I released my breath and selfish musings. Only guilt for not previously sharing in her joy washed over me. "I'm not angry with you. Chadwick is a good man. You couldn't find better. He'll be not only a good husband but a good father." I clasped my hands.

Gratitude filled her eyes. "I love him very much. He's wonderful. And he truly loves the boys. I'm so delighted they'll have a father to look after them."

"This is wonderful, Maggie, but I do have a concern."

She gave her head a confused shake. "What is wrong?"

I hesitated. "I do not want you to leave me," I finally admitted. "I would miss you terribly."

"Is that your worry?" She laughed with relief. "Of course, I shall stay! Just as will Chadwick."

"You shall stay?" I could hardly contain my relief.

"Chadwick has already received permission from your brother."

"I'm surprised *Maman* did not share that news."

Maggie looked away, as if she knew the reason, but didn't want to tell me.

I cleared my throat to push away the tears that were threatening to come. Of course, *Maman* knew that I would be envious of Maggie's happiness.

"Adela has been wonderful. She's given us permission to move into the cottage by the pond. She insists that we invite our families to a supper after the wedding on the terrace."

"What family?" I blurted out before thinking. As soon as I spoke, I knew I should have been more sensitive. She had a brother . . . and a father. No matter how badly the man had treated her, he was still her father.

"Well, you are my family now," Maggie spoke softly. "But I do have some hope . . . there are rumors in the village that my father is doing better. Surely, he knows I'm here at Reigate."

I stepped closer and took her hand. "Perhaps he truly is better now," I said not believing it, but it felt good to reach out to someone who hurt, forgetting for a moment my own.

When Maggie left, fatigue took me to my bed. I'd closed the curtains, blocking out the sunshine. I thought about changes and how life circled around me—Maggie getting married, Adela expecting a child, William being our master—and I was in the center, unmoving and alone. Waiting for this pain to leave.

CHAPTER TWENTY-ONE

Exhausted from Christmas events, I lounged in the solar with William and *Maman*. Being with child, Adela retired early. A fire burned low, the coals glowing red. I stared at them in my fatigue.

Before dawn, we had gathered in the chapel for mass, signaling the end of Advent and the start of the feasting season. The day continued with gift exchanges and a merry feast. *Maman* arranged for the servants and tenants to enjoy dancing and games while we watched. It had always been my favorite time of year. But now was also the time when I thought more of *Père*, missing his presence. And perhaps presents, for he always gave such thoughtful gifts.

And what was Henry doing this night? Did he think of me anymore or believe all was lost and had moved on with his life?

William sipped a warm caudle, then set it aside. "The talk this day was of the battles in the North—in Yorkshire—between the English and the Scots. The battles were led by King David himself, his son at his side."

My weariness forgotten, I sat upright. "How does Henry fare?"

"Must we talk of this at the end of a glorious day?" *Maman* said gloomily.

William ignored *Maman* and gave me a quizzical look. "He's alive if that's what you need to know. But Ada, he is now our enemy. He has killed women and children."

"He has not. I do not believe it." I stuck out my chin and glared at William.

"I have it on reliable word that the Scots slaughtered people of both sexes and every age and rank. They destroyed, pillaged, and burned churches and houses, obliterating whole towns." William's jaw clenched so hard it rippled.

I wanted to cover my ears. "Lies. All lies." Tears burned my eyes.

"Believe it, sister. There are also tales of the Scots carrying off women and children as slaves."

That I could believe, for it was done on all sides in war, England included.

"King David is in support of his niece Empress Matilda's claim to the English throne."

"His judgment stands to reason," I said.

"But he attacked when he knew King Stephen was in the South. Our king could only send a small force to Yorkshire."

King David was a strategist, and Henry had warned me this would happen. It should not have taken anyone by surprise.

William leaned forward, putting his forearms on his knees. "Archbishop Thurston of York raised an army, preaching that to withstand the Scots was to follow God. He mounted a standard on a cart, bearing a pyx carrying the consecrated host."

This troubled me. "It is a dangerous thing to bring God into war and should be heresy to claim to know the mind of Him, our Holy Father." I clasped the cross hanging at my neck.

"Is your allegiance to Scotland then? Do you not follow an archbishop even?"

"Do not put words in my mouth, brother. I follow God, and He would not condone war."

William sat back and raked his hand through his hair, then turned to *Maman.* "Whether we had God's support or not, nearly ten thousand Scots fell. What are your thoughts on the matter, *Maman?*"

Ten thousand? My stomach turned to stone. "*Non!*" Burning tears fell.

Maman stood and came to me, sitting at my side, taking my hand in hers. "This is proof that Scots are barbaric, as I've told you before. I'm relieved I could never agree to you marrying Prince Henry. If your father were alive, he would now say the same."

I pulled my hand from *Maman's* and stood. "You are all wrong. You don't know Prince Henry like I do. False rumors carry from Yorkshire to here, changing and growing along the route. Those who are the victors create their own kind of truth, exaggerating how or why they won, convincing themselves they are the righteous and choicest rulers."

William stood too. "You are speaking traitorous words. I fight on battlefields for England. In your heart, you must do the same."

Through the years, I had many times told myself I could not marry Henry, but then my experiences at court had given me hope. Now it was more than clear there was no possible way for the match. He was my enemy.

So, how could I still care for him so much? My love had not changed in all these months.

CHAPTER TWENTY-TWO

Anno Domini early 1139
Reigate Castle

One overcast afternoon, I sat with *Maman* and William behind the closed doors of William's apartment. The request to join them had been formal, and I feared the conversation they wished to have.

Outside, a flash of lightning brightened the room, and in seconds, rain pattered against the window. An omen of what was to come?

"King Stephen has requested that your hand be given in marriage." William came directly to the point, as he was so apt to do.

On one hand, I was grateful that he had wasted no time, on the other hand, his words sent my mind spinning. I was a lamb to be bartered and bought.

"He has assured me that the union is advantageous to the strength of his kingdom." My brother's forceful tone left me no doubt that the decision had already been made, and I had no choice.

A pawn. The term cut more deeply than ever. "But . . . but I want to marry for love, not political gain." I knew better, but I couldn't accept it without fighting for myself.

William scowled.

Maman patted my hand. "*Mon chéri*, it's rare that love comes before marriage. But it can come with time."

Tears flowed down my cheeks. I clenched my fists and tried to keep my temper at bay. "Do you not care or respect me enough to ask my opinion or give me a choice? Who is this man I am to marry?"

William clenched his jaw, obviously agitated. "You are being obstinate. You know we are beholden to the king. People who question or stand up to him have titles stripped, lands taken, and are imprisoned or killed."

Maman and William eyed each other as if silently quarreling about which of them must deliver the next news. Finally, William stood and walked toward the window.

Maman cleared her throat, then squeezed my hand. "The negotiations have been completed. The king has decided on a nobleman with a great title. He is Marquess Elmund de Bourgogne. Quite wealthy, and he has many homes in France."

I could no longer stay seated. Pulling my hand away from *Maman*, I moved to stand between my brother and the window, where I could not be ignored. "You oblige me to leave England— perhaps to never see you again? You would do this to your own sister?"

"You haven't broken her of these silly romantic notions?" he said to *Maman*. "Why would she believe she has a say? What foolishness have you allowed to sprout here? She's already old . . . She's lucky the king is making a match for her as it is."

"Of course, she will obey the king. Just give her a moment." *Maman* came and put her arm around me. She gave no comfort. She never wanted me to marry a Scot and this solved that problem in her eyes.

"How old is he?" I wanted the answer. And didn't.

She squeezed my shoulders. "Forty-three. He has been married twice and has six children. He is a distant cousin of mine. I know him to be a kind man."

I supposed he could be older. But children? I had not reckoned that. So, I would become an instant mother. They could be my age or older for all I knew. My stomach soured.

"Ada, do not be afraid to grow up and become a woman," my mother said. "I'm sure you will not be so far away. There will most certainly be visits to Reigate. And we will surely come to you. I am due for a visit to my homeland."

I could not contain the tears—they flowed nearly as heavily as the rain on the windowpane. "But I want my marriage to have the kind of love that you and *Père* had." I looked at my brother, who refused to look at me. "And what you and Adela have too."

William finally looked at me. His countenance softened. "Very few nobles have the luxury of marrying for love. You must do your duty. *Père* would have told you the same."

"At least I knew *Père* cared about what happened to me," I said through a tight throat.

William grimaced but didn't negate the accusation. With hands clenched, he left the room.

I wasn't upset that I'd at least caused him a little bit of pain. My tears continued to flow.

"You must forget Henry." *Maman* stood beside me, compassionate, but trembling slightly. Was she unsure of this match? "You are ordained by God to marry whomever the king has chosen for you for the good of our country. This union helps solidify peace between our countries. Do you not want to do that for all of us?" She stepped in front of me and touched my arm. "Can you not understand?"

Ordained by God? "God has nothing to do with this!" I stared at my mother in disbelief—the one person who might understand, yet she didn't. And for the first time in my life, I felt estranged from her.

I yanked my arm from her grasp and ran outside into the storm. I had no care to hold up my tunic, even though the mud would ruin it. I pulled at my braids, untangling them from bondage. *Bondage.* So much like my life, burdened with obedience to the responsibilities of nobility. I wanted freedom to choose what to do. Freedom to give my heart in marriage to whomever I wished.

Henry, why did you not come for me?

"Where is Cooper?" I shouted, entering the stable.

Maggie looked up from the hay pile where she sat playing with the twins. The three of them stared at me. She stood. "M'lady, whatever is the matter?"

Chadwick came from inside a stall. "But 'tis raining, m'lady."

I shoved my dripping hair aside. "I'm already wet. Do as I ask and prepare my horse!"

His eyes widened, then deepened into hurt. But he saddled Cooper.

I mounted with a fury and started off to my land—the land I loved. Rain whipped in my face as I rode with no thought of direction. Cooper turned toward the forest. Thick underbrush in the deep woods forced me to slow.

For the second time in my life, my heart felt as if it was literally breaking. The pain in my chest caused me to bend forward. Tears mixed with the raindrops. The confusion, the hurt, and the fear I'd carried my entire life poured out of me.

"Why am I not allowed control of my own life?" I shouted to the trees, to God, to this place I had always come for comfort. "How can I accept that I was born to marry at someone else's will? And why, why was I given a taste, even a small taste, of what life might be like with Henry?"

Some pain lifted from my soul in the simple act of uttering my despair, of giving voice to my anguish, and directing it toward God.

The rain calmed to a drizzle, and Cooper continued walking slowly through the woods. After several minutes, the rain stopped completely, and the sun broke through the clouds. Rays of light illuminated the trees and began to warm me.

Over the months I'd sent up hundreds of prayers begging God for Henry to be in my life. But now I wanted to pray—to *really* pray.

I remembered back to a time as a young girl when I was afraid a hobgoblin had visited me in one of the many caverns on our land. Gundred had said to me then, "I suggest we calm your soul by visiting the chapel." She took my hand as we walked to the small structure on a rise, built for my family's private worship and ceremonies.

We climbed the stairs and entered through ornate stone arches leading into the cool and quiet nave. Our slippers clicked and echoed against the floor and walls. It smelled like the remnants of tallow candles. Entering the chancel through an intricately carved rood screen, we came to the sanctuary where Gundred released my hand and knelt before the stone altar backed by the east wall.

I knelt beside her and glanced her way uncomfortably, but she had already clasped her hands and bowed her head. Praying inside a cold chapel had no appeal to me. I'd never come this far into the church before, but had always remained in a pew, listening to the priest's sermons, *Maman* giving me stern stares to remind me to sit still.

A small wooden statue of Christ sat at the altar's center, with unlit candles on either side. We had no firesticks to light the candles, but it appeared to be no matter to Gundred's worship. The sunlight shone on her bowed head through purples, reds, and golds of stained-glass in front of us. The colored glass depicted Christ in His majesty, seated on His throne, red robes flowing around him. Winged angels hovered on either side. I took a deep breath and tried to understand the importance of the Savior to Gundred, who always talked as if He were her friend.

Had all the daily prayers offered here been heard by God? He felt distant and uncaring to me. Gundred broke the silence and prayed vocally in Latin, as if the words easily left her tongue. Maybe I needed to spend more time on my knees for God to hear me?

Then Gundred's words stopped but her lips kept moving. What prayers did she offer? Was she asking God to help her cope with the stranger she was soon to wed?

I copied her and clasped my hands, but when I closed my eyes, I found I didn't know what to pray for. Clare had always said a prayer at my bedside at night after she tucked me in. Do I just say words like I would if God stood before me? At the thought of Him actually being in the chapel, my eyes popped open, and I looked around, seeing no one. If He were here, he'd know how I'd stolen from the kitchen, or all the times I was angry at Gundred or my brothers. Thankfully, Gundred stood and so could I. I hurried from the chancel, down the nave and out into the sunshine.

Gundred caught up to me. "I prayed you'd find comfort when I left for my new home."

I never thought she'd be praying for me. A lump suddenly formed in my throat. I wrapped my arms around her waist and cried while she rubbed my back and soothed my sadness.

I needed Gundred now. I needed her comfort and prayers.

Cooper and I came to a cavern, and I slid off him. Entering, I found a dry place and knelt. It wasn't a chapel and I'd long since grown out of believing in hobgoblins, but it was a quiet and private place to speak to God.

"Oh God, if you are there, I plead with you to help me. I'm powerless as to my fate. Guide me to what is best for my life. Gundy always said we each have a purpose to fulfill. Hear my supplication that you show me mine. And I solicit thy peace, I pray."

Waiting in silence for a few moments, I listened, not sure how I should expect to hear an answer. No voice boomed back at me. No angel appeared. But somehow, I felt a small glimmer of hope.

I thought of the carved sparrow the queen—Henry?—had sent me. Hope!

I stood, gathered my skirts, and left the cavern. Knowing Cooper would follow, I walked on through the deep woods, gazing up as the breeze caressed the leaves and treetops. The sound of the wind comforted, and a new sensation of love and peace filled me. I placed my hand over my chest, relishing the overwhelming feeling.

As I stepped into a warm beam of sunlight, a distinct impression entered my mind. *I am watching over you, Ada. I love you. You will have much happiness in your life. Do not let your heart be troubled.*

Tears came freely. *God loves me!* He was guiding my life. Even though I did not understand it all now, I knew with Him beside me everything would turn out all right.

The afternoon quickly gave way to twilight. I said one more prayer for faith—faith to live my life with grace and purpose as King Stephen and my brother wished. To become the woman my mother had raised me to be.

CHAPTER TWENTY-THREE

Anno Domini 1139
Late Spring at Westminster Palace

"Ada, we must be leaving!" *Maman's* voice grew impatient through the door. For the last hour, she'd been trying to get me to come down and board the covered cart that would take us to London.

I took a final look around the room I'd cherished for seventeen years. My eyes lingered on my image in the glass. I looked different with my hair arranged in soft curls to my waist and one of *Maman's* hair clasps tucked in the side near my ear. The French imported, soft-green tunic I wore fell to the floor with an elegant train in the back. It was a suitable dress for my arrival at Westminster Palace— where King Stephen would greet me, and I'd meet my fate with Marquess Elmund de Bourgogne.

Maman opened my door and peeked inside. "William and Adela are ready."

"I fear I'm leaving something behind." I would never come back to this house as a single woman and probably never sleep in this chamber again. It was all too much. How could I be happy in France?

"No matter now. We must be on our way." She took my hand and led me through the door. "I can send you whatever you feel you'll need in your new home."

I looked back one last time, then followed her down the stairs to the two gilded carts prepared for our journey.

Maggie, holding my mantle over her arms, stood waiting.

Six of William's knights in uniform sat mounted and ready to escort us to London.

Maman, Maggie, and I settled into the first cart and Adela, William, and Reginald in the one behind. Our entourage started away. Driving through Reigate's grounds, I silently said goodbye to my childhood and the land I loved—the castle, the trees, and finally the pond. The ducks and swans seemed to watch my departure in silent remorse at my leaving.

Oh, to dream one more hour beside that pond. How many times had I sat staring at the spot where I'd first laid eyes on Henry? How often had I prayed he would ride his horse out of those trees one more time?

But I must give up those childhood fantasies. The time had come to do my duty. The king was calling for his pawn, his strategy already in motion. Like the pawn, I could only move forward. I'd no choice but to fulfill his bidding. Why not do it willingly as Gundred had?

The journey was both painfully long and altogether too short. The countryside rolled by, each bump of the cart bringing me nearer to what I feared most. Try as I might, I could not keep my thoughts from wandering northward.

Had Henry forgotten me? Did he ever think about our time together in the gardens at Westminster? It was so long ago when he'd promised to be my champion should I need him at court. I longed to send word to him now, but by the time a messenger reached him, it would be too late.

Westminster Palace's majestic towers rose above the rooftops, its sand-colored limestone gleaming in the sunshine. Colorful flags lined the path beyond the gates, and pennants hung from the low eaves, fluttering in the wind.

Legion trumpeters on horses, arrayed in red and gold caparisons, lined the front entrance to the palace. On signal by their leader, they raised trumps to their lips and played a welcoming fanfare.

King Stephen approached on his horse, accompanied by two attendants. The sight of him recalled all the emotions of our last encounter. I'd not seen him since that terrible day when he had pitted my brother against my love and failed to let Henry declare who he wanted for a wife.

"Greetings and welcome!" the king called out. He dismounted and came toward us as we alighted from our cart.

Maman curtsied. "It is an honor, King Stephen."

"The honor is mine," he responded with beaming eyes and a smile of regal satisfaction. His voice seemed different somehow— almost as if his kindness were sincere. "I'm pleased to see you, my dear Lady Ada." He took my hand. "You have become a powerful asset to your king. This match will be remembered throughout history."

His words sent an unwelcome shiver through me. A powerful asset was simply another way of saying I was a pawn. I withdrew my hand from his grasp and looked beyond him to the palace entrance. "My king, where is my betrothed?"

"He's not ready to greet you."

I grimaced, wishing to end the torture of anticipation.

The king chuckled. "Not long ago that would have been good news to you. And now you are concerned? Fear not, you'll see your future husband soon enough."

"When am I to wed, Sire?" I asked, my voice nearly quaking.

King Stephen turned to my mother and raised an eyebrow, then looked back at me. "I must admit that I did not anticipate that you'd be in a hurry."

The second cart came to a halt behind us, and William emerged. He offered Adela his hand as she stepped down, then turned to the king. "Your Majesty." They gave low bows.

"William, young Earl of Surrey." The king greeted my brother with a slap on the back. "I must say I'm quite disappointed in you. You had me believe that your sister was hesitant." He smiled at me. "I'm well pleased that she desires to carry out her king's wishes swiftly."

I opened my mouth, wanting desperately to protest, but William's icy stare stopped me.

King Stephen offered an arm to me and the other to *Maman*.

The trumpeters played on, and we walked toward the palace entrance. With all my heart, I wished I could turn and run.

"The queen and your future husband will meet us later in the Great Hall." King Stephen explained. "She has just returned from Durham."

Durham was in the north. What had the queen been doing there? Stephen's forces had been battling the Empress Matilda's armies in France for some months. I'd heard William telling *Maman* that King Stephen himself had been fighting there with his troops and had only recently returned. My wedding would help seal an alliance with France.

"What news?" William asked. "Were the queen's negotiations successful?"

"The loss of Northumberland is significant, but we will retain Bamburg and Newcastle," King Stephen replied. "It's a small price to pay to stop the bloodshed."

"You have reached a treaty then?" William asked.

"My queen has performed her duties well, and for the present, we are no longer in danger."

A strange feeling of elation and hope rushed through me. Could they be talking of a treaty with Scotland? Dare I hope that our countries were no longer at war? I longed to ask for news of Henry, but I feared reigniting the king's wrath toward him. And yet, if our countries were no longer at war, there might be hope that Henry would come back to court.

Perhaps I could inquire of the queen if I had a moment to speak with her. But these were ridiculous thoughts. Even now the Marquess de Bourgogne prepared to meet me.

Upon entering the palace, we were shown to the chambers where our belongings had been delivered and servants waited. They wasted no time getting us unpacked and settled.

When *Maman* and I were finally alone, she stood quietly at the window, looking out.

I went to her and embraced her from behind.

She set her hands on mine. "I wish *ton père* could be here with us. He'd be so proud of you." She looked over her shoulder at me with tear-filled eyes. "My home will feel empty when you're gone."

Her words only compounded my pain.

"I found you!" Gundred burst into the room and hurried to us, her blue eyes vibrant, her stomach large with child. "What are these tears? Must we carry on the tradition of crying at weddings?" She put her arms around us. "Such an old-fashioned custom on a happy occasion."

Realizing this was one of my last meetings with her for quite some time, since I was to leave England after my wedding, I became overcome with emotion. Knowing nothing of my future was insufferable—each moment of uncertainty an agony.

A light knock came at the door. Maggie entered. "My ladies, you are being summoned to the Great Hall."

"Are you ready?" Gundred asked.

I sucked in a deep breath. "Is one ever ready for such a meeting?" I was to meet the man who held my future. Was he kind or cruel? Attentive or aloof?

She took my hand, and we started toward the door.

"Wait a moment," *Maman* called us back. "I may not have another chance to talk alone with Ada. Come sit." She patted a chair.

159

"But *Maman*, they are waiting." Gundred pursed her lips.

I was more than happy to forestall the inevitable meeting.

"It has been a long tradition in my family for the mother of the bride to have her say." She patted the chair again. "Now come sit."

I held back tears. How I wished we were having this conversation under different circumstances. I wanted this special time with *Maman*, but nothing about this day felt special. The man I was to call my husband would have to wait a little longer. Obediently, I sat on the chair.

Gundred quietly slipped out the door.

Maman looked into my eyes. "Now that you will become a bride, resolve to do all you can to bring your husband happiness. It will ensure your own happiness. Will you promise?"

I lowered my eyes. "I will do everything in my power, *Maman*. Is that all you have to say?" I started to stand.

She put her hand on my shoulder and gently pushed me back into the chair. "Take your promise seriously, Ada. You talk so much about the unfairness of marrying a man you don't love, but do you realize you *can* love him? And he you?"

I inhaled deeply and nodded. Taking her hands in mine, I pulled her up, then gave her a loving embrace. "I promise to try and bring my husband happiness."

Maggie cleared her throat.

I had not realized she stood nearby.

"Let me assure you," Maggie said, motioning us toward the door. "When dealing with men, it takes true devotion to keep *that* promise."

Maman and I laughed at Maggie with her "many years" of marital expertise and followed her down the tapestry-lined hallway.

Entering the Great Hall where minstrels played, we found William and Adela, Gundred and Roger, and a sea of unknown faces. The room vibrated with chatter.

I scrutinized each man intently. None distinguished himself above the others. I could not imagine uniting myself in marriage to any of them.

William turned toward two of the men. "Allow me to introduce Johannes de La Trésoille from France and Baron Hefni Van Hoesbroek from Denmark."

I returned the men's bows with a curtsy.

My brother then gestured toward two men and a woman standing close by. "I believe you know Sir Hugh Giffard and Sir Alexander St Martin—and his wife, Sybil."

The faces seemed familiar. "Of course. We are acquainted." I must have met them when we came to Westminster last year. Or perhaps these were men who'd fought alongside my father. That must be it.

As Gundred and *Maman* greeted them, I searched the room again. *Who is he? Where is he?*

My search was interrupted by the bellman announcing the queen's entrance.

The room fell silent as she made her way to the throne, surrounded by her attendants, all of us bowing. Once seated, she smiled and beckoned me to join her.

"Please excuse me," I said to the others.

"Of course." *Maman* gently guided me toward the queen. She let go before we reached the throne.

I walked the last few steps alone, no longer feeling like a girl but a grown woman who served her country by obediently following royal command.

"Ada, my darling, come sit just below me, here." The queen motioned to the step below her, and I was instantly reminded of when she interviewed me a year ago.

I curtsied and obeyed.

"I believe you've grown even more enchanting since I last beheld you."

"*Merci*," I uttered softly. My heart pounded hard in my chest, and I wondered if I would have enough courage to ask about Henry. Surely, she would have heard word of him when she was negotiating the treaty in the North. Perhaps she'd even seen him.

The smile faded from the queen's lips. "Are you quite well? You seem troubled."

I took a deep breath, trying to summon an ounce of bravery. "Your Highness, I fear I only have a few moments with you, and I must ask . . ." I lowered my voice. "Have you heard word of Prince Henry? Is he well?"

The queen took my hands and squeezed them. "'Tis so good of you to ask about my cousin. I have, in fact, beheld him with my own eyes. And I can assure you he is quite well." Her Scottish accent comforted me, reminding me of Henry. It was heartening that others would always love him even if I couldn't.

"Was he at Durham?" I asked, hoping she'd give more details.

She nodded. "He was. And played a vital role in negotiating peace. My uncle, David King of the Scots, has always been most stubborn and unreasonable."

"Do you think the peace will last this time?"

The queen squeezed my hands again, then released them. "I have great hope that it will."

CHAPTER TWENTY-FOUR

Moments later, the bellman announced the king.

I stood and bowed, as did everyone else in the room.

I fully expected to see my betrothed walk in with King Stephen, but to my surprise, the king entered alone. The anticipation too much to bear, the room closed in around me.

The king did not stop to greet others but made his way directly to the throne.

My time alone with the queen was drawing to a close.

"Has Prince Henry . . ." I hesitated.

"Aye?" she asked.

"Has he taken a bride?"

The queen glanced at me and smiled sympathetically. "Not yet," she whispered, rising up from her throne to greet her husband.

Her smile and those two words lit a fire of hope inside me. Henry was not yet married. Our countries were no longer at war.

I curtsied again as the king approached, my heart nearly pounding out of my chest. I may only be a pawn in the hands of this powerful king, but I would not go quietly. All the resolve I'd mustered through my prayers came forward. Henry had fought a knight's battle for the bride he thought he wanted, even if it wasn't me. Now I must fight for him, a future king. Again, I thought about how the pawn can only move forward. Forward with strategy to win.

"My darling," King Stephen said, reaching for his queen's hand.

She lowered her head, but her eyes stayed fixed on his. The look that passed between them strengthened my resolve. Their marriage had most certainly been the result of a political arrangement, yet love had clearly blossomed between them.

Maman and William would have me trust that this could be the case for me, but how could I make it happen with the intense feelings I had for Henry? Those feelings would not simply melt away because I was being given to another man.

The king turned to me.

I curtsied a third time in my nervousness, "Your Majesty." My lips spoke the required words, but the fire rising inside became impossible to extinguish.

"Ada, you are a feast for the eye." The king took my hand and kissed the back of it. "Your husband is most fortunate to have secured such a beautiful bride. I really must thank you. Your famed beauty was a most powerful bargaining tool—more powerful than lands or riches."

My displeasure exploded, and I pulled my hand away. "I am not a possession." That I'd whispered the words did not diminish their intensity.

Gasps came from a few ladies-in-waiting, close enough to hear my words.

"What did she say?" I heard William ask.

The king's eyes widened. He bent closer, as if he wasn't sure he'd heard me. "Perhaps you misunderstand," he said. "I am thanking you."

"I understood. You are thanking me for being a desired commodity. Something of value that can be traded away."

"Ada—" The queen put her hand in front of me, probably trying to protect me from myself, but the gate had been opened, and I couldn't hold back what had been contained inside.

I stepped away from the queen's hand. "My king," I continued in a voice that rang out above the soft music of the minstrels. "I am a person with feelings, desires, and my own will. I know that it is my duty, as your subject, to obey, but in this thing, I simply must speak." I could be put to death for disobeying the king. Why did my emotions put me in such a danger?

"But Ada, you must understand something—" the queen began.

"You are arguing with me?" The words strained through King Stephen's gritted teeth and drew the gasps of those around us.

I turned to Queen Matilda. "*Merci*, my queen." I pled with my eyes for her to forgive me. "You have always had a kind regard for my feelings. I know that you've tried to help, but now I must speak."

The room fell silent.

"All my life I've been taught that it is God's will for me to marry someone who would be chosen for me. I have been taught that love will follow. But Your Majesties," I looked from one to the other. "I cannot become one man's wife when I love another. It will destroy not only my chance at happiness, but that of the man who wishes to purchase my 'famed beauty.'"

The king laughed—the same cackle I remembered from a year ago that had sickened me—only today something in his pitch had changed.

I looked to the queen, trying to understand, to interpret his response.

She laughed too.

From the corner of my eye, I saw my mother moving swiftly in my direction.

William stood frozen with his mouth agape.

The king continued to laugh.

Queen Matilda quickly composed herself. "Ada, my darling, please do not be distressed."

Anger, embarrassment, and confusion swirled inside me. The king's laughter was not unexpected, but I had always supposed the queen to be my ally. Hot tears filled my eyes.

The queen took my hands. "Oh, Ada, you will bring perfect happiness to your husband."

The tears spilled onto my cheeks. "But how can I, when—"

The bellman called out, "Your Royal Majesties."

"Hush now," the queen said. "All is about to become clear."

I turned to the doors along with the entire company to watch my betrothed enter the room.

But Henry stood in the doorway. *Henry.* His brown eyes fixed on me. He took long strides, closing the distance between us.

"May I present the Earl of Huntingdon and Northumberland, Henry Mac David, Prince of Strathclyde." The bellman bowed.

The queen leaned over and whispered in my ear, "Henry was instrumental in helping negotiate peace. King David insisted on the return of the earldom of Northumberland, but Henry only asked for one thing—*You.*"

My breathing stopped and my heart with it. Could it be? Could I truly believe?

Henry halted when he reached the throne and bowed before the king and queen. When he looked up, his eyes were for me. Upon seeing my tears, which still flowed freely, his brows furrowed.

"Prince Henry," King Stephen said. "I'm afraid you'll have your hands full with this one. We couldn't get a word in edgewise to let her know of sudden changes of her future husband. I do not like that she now refuses to obey my wishes. Lady Ada declares that she cannot marry you, for she loves another."

Henry took a step toward me, eyes searching.

I couldn't think clearly, wondering if I should wake from this dream at any moment. My tears continued to fall, but I felt my smile growing wider.

"Lady Ada?" Henry said, with a hint of a grin. "Is this true? Are you in love with another man?"

166

I shook my head vigorously, but somehow words escaped me.

"And would you refuse to obey your king? Would you refuse to be my wife?"

"*Non*," I pushed out. Finally collecting my wits, I dried my eyes and bowed before the king and queen. "Your Majesties—"

"Hush, my dear," the queen mercifully interjected. "You have been apart long enough. Go. Be with your betrothed. Soon you will wed."

With his eyes filled with love, Henry extended his hand.

I didn't hesitate to accept it, my heart thundering in my chest.

We moved quietly out the door, the world melting away as I walked next to Henry, taking him in—his hair had grown longer, the wave more pronounced; there were creases on his face, not just from smiling but surely from the battles he had fought; he moved with confidence. But the feel of my hand engulfed in his made the moment dreamlike. Could this really be happening?

He turned and smiled.

I looked into his eyes and saw only relief and joy. I had so many questions and yet I was content just to be near him, look at him, breathe him in.

He slowed in the hallway and wiped at my tears.

I closed my eyes, relishing his touch. He wanted me. A thrill passed through my entire body.

"Come." Henry tugged my hand. "I know a place where we can be alone."

My heart raced, elated I would have time with him.

After a short distance, he stopped and opened a door to reveal a narrow, spiral staircase. "I discovered this by accident on my last visit."

"Where does it lead?"

"Let me show you." He didn't let go of my hand while we climbed the stone steps.

I brought his hand to my lips and kissed it.

He stopped and turned, a burning in his eyes. Then smiled and pulled my hand to continue ascending the stairs.

Up, up we climbed to the top of a high tower and stepped out into the fading, golden sunlight. The small half-walled area—a guard's watchtower—provided a breathtaking view of the river with the city in the distance, as far as the eye could see were innumerable houses, crowded together, smoke coming from cooking fires.

An ornate cart with golden wheels in the French style hurried out the palace gates. Was it the Marquess de Bourgogne, I wondered? I silently wished him better luck in finding a bride.

I turned away from the sight. "The height is making me dizzy." Or perhaps, Henry's nearness was making me dizzy. I needed to breathe. I still felt utter shock and amazement that I would not be marrying a stranger. That Henry had come for me.

Silent for a moment, he appeared pensive as he surveyed London. "I must admit that when I rode away a year ago, I had little hope that I would ever return to King Stephen's court."

"And I had little hope of ever seeing you again." I softly touched his tunic at his chest, remembering William's lance shattering on Henry's breastplate. "Were you badly hurt? I never asked."

"'Twas a difficult journey home." His attention drifted away.

I embraced his arm to bring him back to me. "I could not help imagining the worst."

He turned fully toward me. "As did I." He brushed his thumb lightly over my cheek and I relished his skin touching mine. "I feared King Stephen would see you married before I could come back for you. Fortunately, he was wise enough to keep you as a bargaining tool."

A frown pulled at my mouth. "His pawn."

"I never intended for you to be forced." He brushed his fingers across my jaw. "I promised you all those years ago that I would be your champion. I wanted this to be your choice, but when the queen told me the king decided to marry you to a Frenchman, I knew I had to act."

"What would have happened if England and Scotland hadn't been in need of a treaty when they did? You almost lost me."

"I'd hoped to hear that you refused the Frenchman."

I couldn't contain my laughter. "I did. Right before you walked in the room, I told the king I could not marry a stranger when I loved someone else."

His hand stilled on my jaw. "Say it again." Henry tilted my chin upward until I was looking in his eyes.

"I love you, Henry."

"I love you too, dear Ada." He kissed my forehead, then his lips were near my ear and I shivered. "I realize the decision has been made for us, but do *you* wish to marry me? I've longed to hear your response."

Since childhood, understanding I was to be a pawn for my country, Henry's words were all I ever longed to hear. My heart and soul were completely his. "Aye, dear Henry. I—"

The door opened, and a surprised guard stepped out. "What . . .?"

Henry moved away and I instantly felt the loss of a pivotal moment.

"We were just leaving." He took my hand and squeezed, leading me back down the stairwell. "Shall we visit the gardens?" he said with a gleam in his eye.

"That would be lovely." I took in a deep breath, longing for another intimate moment like the last. Could this really be my future? A life with the man I loved. It was going to take some time to believe I wasn't in some kind of dream.

Hand in hand in the garden, we walked for a time without speaking, simply enjoying our closeness while surrounded by beauty. The gardens were in spring bloom—bright yellow daffodils, anemones, irises, and crocus of all colors. But when we came to patches of wildflowers, they brought back memories, and I laughed.

"What is the jest?" Henry inquired.

169

"Oh, it's nothing."

"'Nothing' could bring such a smile to those beautiful eyes?" He stopped and turned me to face him. "Tell me what's going on inside your lovely head."

"It's the wildflowers." I picked a purple violet. "As a child, I used to gather fists full of these from our fields whilst imagining I was marrying a handsome prince—of my choice—whom I loved. It was a childish fantasy." I held the flower to his nose.

He took in a deep breath.

"And yet, my fantasy has become reality."

He smiled and pushed a lock of hair away from my face. Then he took the flower and placed it above my ear. "It pleases me to be the prince of your fantasies." Pulling me close, he pressed his lips against mine. The kiss so like the ones shared in these same gardens a year before. It left me breathless.

We continued to wander the gardens in silence. I didn't want the magic of our time together to end, but the sun had set and the last of its light faded, leaving a thin golden glow on the horizon.

"Ada, I need to hear you say it, will you stand by me? I need your reassuring support." He took my hands in his. "Before our wedding, I'll meet with King Stephen and other officials of England and Scotland to go over the terms of the Treaty of Durham. Yet, I'm apprehensive."

"But why?"

He dropped my hands and paced a few steps. "It's a significant change for Scotland. It lends more security to our shared borders, but it also pledges Scotland's support in fighting mutual enemies and confirming existing alliances."

I shook my head. "How can that be bad?"

"My father has some loyalties to Empress Matilda. He spent his youth training in the courts of King Henry. The war with the empress isn't over, and many Scots don't want to fight for England. The treaty binds us to obligations with King Stephen."

I understood the reality of his fears. "Whatever happens"—I gripped his hand—"I will support you."

He kissed my fingertips. "I've always liked your strength and should have known you were made to be a queen."

I stepped closer and looked into his face. "I love you, Henry."

"I love you, my darling", he whispered. He leaned in slowly and kissed me again.

In that kiss I felt the strength of companionship. Neither of us would be alone again.

Still holding my hand, he walked me past an elegant statue of the Madonna and Child. We sat on a stone bench that looked over the river Thames. "Before you take the role of my wife and future Queen of Scots, I feel I need to remind you that there will always be danger in our lives."

I nodded having considered this many times since we last spoke of it. "I understand. I am not going to be your lover only. I am going to support you in all things."

He smiled that lopsided grin, then kissed my fingers but soon worry creased his brow again. "It's not only the descendants of Scottish kings that are a threat to us, but others who are angry with the royal family. Ranulf de Gernon, Earl of Chester, for one. He's outraged and gathering an army against me as we speak."

"But why?" The threat suddenly became very real. An army against Henry!

"King Stephen gave my father estates in treaty that he'd previously given to Ranulf's father. Ranulf has sworn to stop at nothing to regain his lands. I shudder to think what that may mean."

After a moment of silence, Henry stood, pulled me to my feet, and led me a short distance to stand beneath the arch of the rose arbor. "You're young and innocent, sheltered from trouble all your life. I wish our lot were not such, but 'tis so. I must know you are willing to accept these things. And at the same time I am sorry—so sorry—to ask."

I remembered what God told me after my prayer in the cavern—to not let my heart be troubled. God knew all along my future would be with Henry and with his people. I would leave Reigate, but I was going to a new home with the man I loved, who loved me too. No one chose him for me but myself. And God. "I was raised to serve. I pledge my life to you and your country. I stand by you now, and I will never step away."

CHAPTER TWENTY-FIVE

Waiting another week for Henry's countrymen and family to gather in London, the day finally came for our wedding. *Maman* and Gundred came hours before to help me make ready.

I was so anxious, I couldn't sit or stand still and instead took to pacing the floor. I hadn't stopped thinking about the worries Henry had shared with me. I remembered him telling me there were many Englishmen who didn't want a Scot as their lord, but his inherited English lands from his mother's family were where we were going to live after the wedding.

"Calm yourself, my lady. All will be well." Maggie laid out my wedding tunic on the bed.

Gundred touched the imported silk of the dress, as blue as the Reigate sky. "It's so soft, so perfect! And look, the seal of Warenne is on the overlay with its blue-and-gold checkered design. You'll be stunning."

I slowed my stride long enough to gaze upon the seal. "I requested it, wanting some way to honor *Père* and our heritage." I looped my arm through *Maman's*. "Maggie did a splendid job with the embroidery."

173

I peeked over at Maggie, who bustled with preparations as though she hadn't heard the compliment. She failed at her attempt to hide a pleased smile before ducking from the room.

"The emblem is not solely his," *Maman* said with a touch of defensiveness in her voice. "When your father and I married, he adopted my family's seal of the Vermandois Coat of Arms as his own. The blue-and-yellow checks became known as the Warenne *chequer*."

I stroked the embroidery momentarily, then resumed my pacing. Walking was the only way to relieve my nervous energy. "Then I honor both of you, the Vermandois and the Warennes, on this day."

I turned to *Maman*. "I know you did not want me to marry a Scot. Tell me I have your best wishes."

She smiled sadly and nodded once. "Because of your love for him and how happy I've seen you this past week, I have come to a sort of peace. And besides"—she shrugged—"You are now obeying your king."

I kissed her on the cheek.

Maggie returned to the chamber and laid a pale-blue cloak beside the dress.

Gundred looked at me with admiration. "With Henry in his ceremonial robes and crown, you and he will be a stunning couple."

Mother admired the handiwork. "Oh Maggie, I'll miss you and your talents when you go with Ada to Northumbria."

"What?" I choked on the word.

Maman smiled, almost laughing. "Maggie, Chadwick, and the twins will join you in Northumberland as soon as they can."

My eyes instantly welled with tears. "Oh, *Maman*! *Merci*."

Maman gave a gentle squeeze of my hands as she often did when I needed calming. "Stop fidgeting and hold still," she whispered. She turned and lifted something off the table, and opened a box lined with blue velvet. She lifted out a magnificent gold crown.

Delicate scrolling wound along the banding, and rubies and diamonds set deep within dozens of *fleurs-de-lis*.

Gundred stepped closer. "Lovely!"

I had never seen anything more beautiful. "I'll wear it with pride, *Maman*. You are so good to me." I hugged her.

Later, we arrived at the entrance to Westminster Palace and escorted through the cheering crowds to the top of the palace steps. There we awaited the signal for the ceremony to begin.

My stomach fluttered as if butterflies were within.

Henry stood near the doors with his father. Even at a distance, his eyes were only for me, and I smiled at him. He wore a purple robe bearing the Saltire of Scotland—St. Andrew's Cross and his own gold crown.

Many of my family—siblings, uncles, aunts, nieces, nephews, cousins—waited with us on the steps. The young boys wore black tunics and stockings and the girls bright frocks with matching ribbons streaming from garlands of fresh flowers laced into their expertly coifed hair.

Accompanied by trumpeters, the magnificent doors of Westminster Palace opened, and Archbishop Theobald de Bec came forward.

The crowd quieted.

The archbishop stood before me. "Lady Ada de Warenne, someday you will become the Queen of Scots. Do you promise to honor Christ and strive for His grace in all you do in your responsibilities of caring for mankind?"

"I do." The weight of my station descended upon me. *God, be with me. You are my first sovereign. Help me be a strong and faithful woman.*

The trumpeters played again, and the throngs cheered.

I tried to remember to breathe.

The archbishop turned and led the way into the palace with my family following behind. The children before me joyously strew flower petals while ill-trying to maintain reverence.

As I neared Henry at the door, he reached for my hand. When our skin connected, it gave me strength and I felt with a surety that God sanctioned our union. He had been in my life all along.

We followed the children down the path of petals through the Great Hall and into Saint Stephens Chapel. Passing honored nobles and guests—including King David, King Stephen, and Queen Matilda—we stepped to where the archbishop awaited us.

We knelt on cushions embroidered with colorful motifs. Throughout the ceremony, I couldn't control my shaking hands. Near the end, I had enough presence of mind to look into Henry's handsome face. My heart thudded hard in my chest at his expression of joy.

He slipped a ring onto my finger and raised my hand to kiss the ring as a symbol of our union.

We stood, turned, and bowed to our guests.

Mother's eyes overflowed with tears, and Gundred's smile could have lit the darkest corner of the room. Her husband, Roger, stood next to her.

King Stephen came to us and held up his hand toward the gathering. "Blessed be England and her sister Scotland. This day and this marriage have brought us together in peace for the good of our countries. I present to you the Royal Highnesses Prince Henry and his beautiful wife, Princess Ada of Scotland!"

Everyone burst into cheers and applause.

After the ceremony, we greeted our guests in the Great Hall as the servants brought in tables. On each, they placed fresh flowers arranged with white and purple heather from Scotland. They scattered peppermint leaves and other herbs amid the rushes to freshen the air. The room filled to overflowing with our countrymen.

At the end of the nuptial feast, Henry stood and lifted his wine goblet. "We are grateful to all who have joined us on this magnificent day. I make a toast to our friendships, your health, and to my lovely bride."

An approving cheer went through the group.

He grasped the handle of a large meat knife and held it high. Its long, pointed, silver blade glinted in the candlelight. "I am a Scot, and the old Gaelic custom is for the betrothed couple to make a small cut on their arms, then press them together to signify a blood union."

A hush fell over the room.

Suddenly uncomfortable, I smiled in disbelief.

Henry took my hand and pulled me to my feet.

Murmurings rippled through the crowd.

The sight of the blade caused perspiration to bead on my forehead.

"But . . . Ada and I will forgo the ritual." He laid the knife on the table and gave me a teasing grin. "We'll seal our marriage with a kiss."

Relief flooded me. I would remember this side of his character. He enjoyed seeing my discomfort and then coming to my rescue. I leaned toward him, expecting a soft, chaste kiss. Instead, his lips lingered in a kiss filled with love.

Our guests pounded on the tables and shouted, "Hurrah!"

Later that evening, as the festivities died down, guests began leaving.

Henry had been talkative all night. We had much to catch up on and learn about each other. I was already weary from the long day when he leaned over and said, "I must meet with King Stephen and our Scottish dignitaries before we retire. I'll join you in the bridal suite shortly, my love."

The moment he left my side, the loss was palpable. I'd already gotten used to him, as if he were the other half of me. I was no longer whole when he wasn't there.

Maman and Gundred walked me to my room, pausing at the door to give me hugs and well-wishes. "We'll see you tomorrow morning," Gundred promised.

Maggie greeted me as I entered. "'Twas a grand wedding party, my lady. You looked beautiful, and more than that, you look content." She winked. "Now, on with the rest of the festivities."

"Oh, Maggie, I'm as nervous as a cat." I looked over the chamber and caught my breath at the sight of the large canopy bed with two linen shifts folded at its foot.

"Shall I bring you a drink of hot wine and herbs to calm your mind?" Maggie asked.

"*Non*, I will be fine," I lied—the flutters in my stomach growing more agitated.

She smiled knowingly. "We have prepared this room for your first night together as man and wife. There is fruit and other tasty morsels over here, including your and Henry's favorites." She pointed to several dishes on the table, one with gingerbread. "And I specially perfumed your bath with rosewater." She went to the fire and removed a heating kettle. She added its contents into the large bathing tub beside the fireplace. Steam rose from the water's surface.

I breathed in, enjoying the scent of roses. "It's lovely." I embraced her after she settled the kettle. "I'm indebted to you for preparing the room with such care."

"For you, only the best." She grinned. "And now, let's get you bathed."

After the bath, I dressed in my shift.

"I'll take my leave, so you may receive your husband properly. May God bless your union." She stepped into the hall and closed the door after her.

I stood before a glass, running a comb through my hair. My thoughts turned back to my vows. To have and to hold, to be meek and obedient . . . the holy Church to ordain. I plight to thee my troth; I give my body that we two may be one.

I glanced down at the stunning ring on my finger, made of blue sapphires that had belonged to Henry's mother, Queen Maud.

When Henry became King of the Scots, I would stand in that great woman's place.

Had this really become my life? It was so much to take in.

I heard shuffling of feet from the hall.

Henry entered the chamber and stared at me with the most distracting smile. How powerful he looked with his height and broad shoulders, his dark hair, and deep-brown eyes. But now, he was not merely a brave knight and warrior, he was *my* brave knight, *my* husband.

He closed the door. "Come, look at my wedding gift to you." He motioned to the ornate wooden trunk at the foot of the bed.

"Did you prepare this for me?" I asked. The distraction helped me relax.

He pulled me close. "Does it please you?" He kissed me on the temple—sweet, warm, promising. "Go ahead. Open it." His breath tickled my ear.

I left his embrace and lifted the lid. A silk tunic lay folded inside, green like a summer meadow. I lifted it out. Embroidered in silver along the hemline was a stunning pattern of birds.

"The swans, robins, sparrows, falcons, and hawks. You remembered!"

He stood behind me, his cheek against mine. "Birds—your favorite animal of Cherchefelle."

"*Merci* with all my heart, *mon cher*. Was the carved sparrow from you then?"

"Aye. It has always been my *hope* that we would wed."

With care, I laid the dress aside and lifted out a golden-yellow cape with white fur lining the edge of the hood. "It's so beautiful!" I slipped it around me. The cloak hung softly to the floor.

Henry reached into the chest for the final items—two jeweled boxes. "These were my mother's, Queen Maud, and my grandmother's, Queen Margaret," he spoke reverently. "One day, you'll join them, Queen Ada."

Queens of the Scots. My eyes filled with tears. "I am honored to stand in such a line." I took the boxes and held them near my heart, trying to connect to these women whose calling and mission I would inherit.

Henry touched one of the boxes. "That was my grandmother's. Open it first."

I lifted the lid and held up a jeweled silver cross etched in intricate design attached to a string of silver beads. The beads draped through my fingers. "I love this, Henry. Such a sacred gift."

"'Twas her personal favorite. My father picked it out for you from a collection of his mother's things." His voice sounded tender and warm.

I'd married a good and gentle man. "I will thank him later." As I laid Margaret's cross on the table, I promised God that He would always be the first I'd go to when making decisions for my new country, just as I was sure Queen Margaret had done. I suddenly remembered the message God gave me that day in the rain—that He watched over me and I would have happiness in life. He was right. Of course, He was right!

I was the most blessed of all women.

I opened the next box. Inside lay a necklace with a teardrop-shaped purple amethyst on a silver loop. I carefully took it out. "This looks like something worn by a queen."

"For my queen."

I held it up to see the flicker of firelight make it gleam. "I love it."

"Now, my Ada." He took the necklace, setting it and the boxes aside. "The night is too short for the joy that I feel. A blessed man am I." He took my hands. "You gave me your heart; I pledge thee my love."

He spoke poetry very much like his wedding vows.

Please God, help me remember this always.

He pulled me to the bedside and kissed me. "I love you, dear Ada."

180

We had married for love. Everything I'd dreamed about, wished for, and prayed for was here in my arms. I had never in my life felt so completely contented.

He kissed me again, then extinguished the candle.

His love emptied my mind of all thought. He kissed in a way that promised a love that would never end.

Our marriage and the Second Treaty of Durham would both be consummated in holy love. England and Scotland could now enjoy peace.

The End

Read the continuation of Prince Henry and Ada de Warenne's story in

A Pawn for a King
Ada de Warenne 1123-1178
Scotland's Princess
Book Two
The Pawn Series
Learn more about Ada de Warenne at
www.sarahhinze.com/books
sarahhinze.hinze@gmail.com

A Sneak Peek

CHAPTER ONE

Anno Domini 1139
The King's Palace at Westminster, London

Clove-covered pinecones crackled in the fireplace, stirring me awake. I smiled. No doubt Henry had ordered them on hearing of my fondness. He had an uncanny knack of noting and attending to the smallest of details—to the woes of his enemies and the delight of those in his favor.

I inhaled deeply, enjoying the pleasing fragrance. Was this a dream? Had I truly wed Prince Henry of the Scots but four months past?

But it wasn't a dream. I'd not dreamed at all last night. A rare occurrence. I dream most nights—dreams of the future and sometimes the past—if there is a lesson to gain. I've learned to not share details, fearing others would think me mad of wit. I alone was aware when my dreams come true.

I reached for my husband. My hand was met with naught but an empty bed and cold linens, *again*. Did Henry never take a proper rest? For an indulgent moment, I sunk my face into his pillow. A pleasant scent greeted me—a blend of leather and pine. It was proof enough that our marriage was real and a reminder to be up and busy myself, looking to my own duties. I sat up, rubbing the sleep from my eyes. A grey hint of the day barely lit the finely crafted shutters, and the bells had not yet sounded for prayers at dawn.

Henry was likely off overseeing details for our departure. I had best be about my own preparations, lest I delay the company. Or worse, they depart without me.

Throwing back the coverlet, my bare feet met the smooth stone floor. I shivered. At all our holdings in England, *Maman* had ordered furs placed at every bedside, both for warmth and comfort. It felt lovely to sink one's toes into the softness. I was surprised King Stephen hadn't thought to do the same here in the palace.

Maman. I'd only been wed a few months and already I was pining for my mother and father. But they were gone. My beloved *Père* had died the year before, and my mother, the great-granddaughter of King Henry I of France, had departed for Normandy after my wedding nuptials were complete.

I worried for her. Ever since Father passed, it was as if she had one foot in this world and the other in the next. How I missed our early morning visits. Ofttimes, she'd slip into my bedchamber before responsibilities of the day weighed heavily upon us. We spoke of trivial matters; advice on my attire, news of the family, humorous blunders made by visitors, menus to be seen too. They were but commonplace exchanges, peppered with laughter and embraces.

Being here without my mother made me realize such simple, stolen moments were the stuff and substance of a happy life. When I had my own daughters someday, I would continue the tradition. This morning, there was no one to chat with about nonsense. The exquisite chamber was as silent as a tomb. Though my heart flowed with love for my new husband, parting from my mother pulled more at my heartstrings than I had expected.

A loud knock at the door startled me.

Likely, it was a servant who came to help me dress. I wrapped myself in a robe and opened the door whilst tying my sash. As I lifted my eyes, heat rose to my face. Henry's cousin stood in the hallway, gazing coolly at me.

Kelton's fine clothing bespoke his position, a great knight of Scotland and a favorite of King Stephen's. Henry had privately explained to me that Kelton was born as a bastard to Henry's uncle, King Alexander, but raised with a noble family. Ever compassionate, Henry had decided to make Kelton steward at our estate in the north. Tall, with dark hair and deep-set brown eyes, the physical similarities to my husband were quite striking. From a distance, one could hardly tell them apart. But the unsettled feeling in my chest stood in sharp contrast to the peace I felt when Henry was nearby.

I lifted my chin. "How may I help you, Kelton?"

"Good morrow, Countess Adaline," he said formally. "I took it upon myself to inform you that we shall soon be ready to depart. I was certain you would not wish to keep the company waiting."

Strange. Any of the servants could have done so. What was Kelton truly about? "*Merci,*" I said. "May I ask where my husband has removed to?"

Something flickered in his eyes. "Prince Henry requested that you not be disturbed." Ignoring my question, he proffered a smile. "I felt sure that your highness would not wish to delay our departure." Bowing with a flourish, he turned to leave. "But, by all means, Countess, take as long as you wish."

He had virtually admitted defiance to my husband's order. I opened my mouth to censure him, then closed it again. As I watched his departing figure, I decided it would not be prudent to antagonize him. Kelton could yet prove to be an ally or at least a source of information. Henry was often so occupied it was proving difficult to keep pace with his doings.

"Excuse me, my lord," I called after Kelton sweetly.

He whirled about. "Aye, Countess?"

My good humor felt strained. I had told him several times that I preferred to be called Ada by my family. He was deliberately seeking to annoy me. Upon my marriage to his cousin, I gained the titles of Countess of Huntingdon and Countess of Northumbria. I suspected he was at ill will with me because I carried a family title by decree of the king.

"Again, *merci* for your thoughtfulness," I said. "It's most appreciated. Have the extra reinforcements Prince Henry expected arrived?"

Kelton hesitated. "At my suggestion, a contingency of our men will meet up with the extra guardsmen. Within a day or so, we shall rejoin the company with greater forces." Again, he had not answered directly.

"*We* will rejoin the company?" I questioned.

"I shall be leading the group," he clarified, his face expressionless. "Have no fear, Countess Adaline. We shall be well fortified before we are exposed to any real danger."

That news brought me no comfort. Our forces would be further reduced over the next several days. Tensions remained high. Stephen's position as the King of England was unsecured at best while Empress Matilda, his cousin and rival, was seeking to take the throne. Forces worked against King Stephen in the south from Normandy. Enemies were everywhere.

185

My new father-in-law, King David of the Scots, had fought for Empress Matilda, opposing Stephen's rise to power, but a new peace treaty had been forged between them, ceasing the hostilities. Part of the agreement between the kings included my marriage to Prince Henry. I had become a pawn for the king.

To ensure compliance with the treaty, my husband, Kelton, and a few others from baronies in the north were under obligation as hostages for a year of service to King Stephen. Hence our stay at the palace in London.

It was for this reason Henry readied himself this morning to follow the king to take Ludlow Castle, near the Welsh borders. I would follow as part of the king's company. So, why would Kelton leave the company more vulnerable at such a dangerous time?

"I will be down shortly." I nodded politely. "If you could be so kind as to give orders for my mount to be saddled, I would be most grateful."

"As you wish, Countess." He touched a finger to his forelock, then strode off down the passageway.

Was Kelton friend or foe to Henry? It was hard to say. I knew so little about those surrounding Henry and who, if any, I could depend upon. There was so much to learn in my new role as a future sovereign's wife. In spite of all my mother's advice and teachings, I hardly knew where to begin. One step at a time, I supposed. I pulled the bell cord to summon a servant to aid in dressing.

She arrived and dressed me in a surcoat. I held a looking glass as she fixed my hair.

"Your hair is beautiful, my lady. And so thick." She sectioned my dark auburn locks into two long plaits.

How Henry loved my hair. In the privacy of our bedchamber, he was particularly fond of loosening my braids and running it through his fingers. I smiled. It pleased me that Henry found my appearance to his liking. "*Merci*. At my mother's insistence, it has never been cut."

"It reaches nearly three-quarters to the floor." She adorned it with ribbons and gold combs and then arranged a wimple and circlet on top of my head. "It's thick enough that there's no need of weaving in horsehair as some of the other fine ladies have me do to add length or fullness."

I stood and adjusted the wimple chin strap. I nodded my appreciation to her. "*Merci.*"

Two housecarls entered the chamber to remove our trunks. I hurried down the wide halls and stairways of Westminster Palace to the chapel for my prayers. When done, I entered the Great Hall and ordered bread and cheese wrapped in a cloth to consume later.

It was in this Great Hall where I'd danced with my father for the last time. I sighed. It was also in this room when I'd learned Henry was to be my husband after months of fearing the king might give me to another. Henry's appearance in the doorway had been my salvation.

"Your bread and cheese, my lady." A servant's voice pulled me back to the present.

"*Merci.*" I took the cloth-wrapped bundle and walked away, still tingling from the memory of Henry's triumphant reappearance in my life.

Read more of Prince Henry and Ada de Warenne's story in

A Pawn for a King:
Ada de Warenne 1123-1178
Scottish Princess
Book Two in The Pawn Series

ACKNOWLEDGEMENTS

Researching and sharing the life of Ada de Warenne, my 25th great grandmother, has been a bonding experience. I now feel I know her and look forward to meeting her with a big hug in the eternities.

I thank all of those who have made contributions to *The English Rose*. First, my husband with whom I have been blessed to know deep love like that of Ada and Henry in this story based on true events. Such love was rare in mediaeval times when marriages were often assigned by kings for political purposes, without regard for love.

Thank you, Brent, for your encouragement and help with travel, research, writing, and editing. (Not to mention your fabulous dishwashing skills when I was laboring on a scene.) You are my prince as Henry was to Ada.

Thanks to other wonderful editors who contributed so much, especially Ora Smith who always goes the extra mile, adding depth and clarity.

Thanks to Lori Freeman for her early editing and advice.

Thanks to Adrienne Quintana who brought this book together in a beautiful package with her Pink Umbrella Publishing Company.

Thanks to my dear friend Kaye Johnson-Janda who read Pawn for a King, and suggested the need for this prequel.

Thank you to Sandi Larsen and the talented team at Eschler Editing who offered heartfelt suggestions in the final stages.

Thank you to beta readers Julia Howard, Audra Powell, Ann Griffin and other dear friends who offered important suggestions such as " give us more about Ada and Henry's meeting, courtship, and how their love developed."

Another special thanks to my friend, screenwriter and author, Jenni James, who gave this book its title in an extraordinary screenplay...*The English Rose*. We believe Ada's story deserves the telling in film as well as in print. (We are prayerfully working on this goal with our fingers crossed!)

Now, from my first Ada book, *A Pawn for a King*, I repeat gratitude to our dear friend and historian, Helen Robertson. To me it was divine intervention when we met in Haddington, Scotland. Helen shared her extraordinary knowledge of medieval events with great generosity, helping to fill in missing links of Ada's life 900 years ago. Helen is the embodiment of going the extra mile, literally, driving Brent and I to sights from Ada's life in Scotland and England. (That's when we learned Helen was a former race car driver! We tightened our seat belts and enjoyed many places and stories we otherwise may have missed.) Thanks to you always, dear Helen.

In conclusion, thanks to our friend (and our daughter's father-in-law), Jim Wyler, who kindly manages my website with his profound computer skills at: www.sarahhinze/books.com

ABOUT THE AUTHOR

Sarah Hinze from Tennessee has collaborated with leading experts on near-death experiences and pre-natal psychology while conducting extensive research and hundreds of interviews. She has published 9 books and presented workshops, seminars, and lectures at conferences and universities, as well as on Capitol Hill and at the United Nations. She has been featured in articles, radio and TV shows in the USA, Canada and Japan. In addition to English, her books have been published in Spanish, Portuguese and German. Her writings and award winning film, *Remembering Heaven,* (available on You Tube) have been a source of healing and hope for individuals worldwide.

Sarah now resides in Arizona with her husband Brent. They are the parents of nine wonderful children and thirty-four amazing grandchildren who lovingly call Sarah "Grandma Waffles" due to the tradition of her famous waffles whenever they come to visit.

The English Rose is book one in a series about Sarah's 25th great grandmother, Ada de Warenne, born about 900 years ago in Surrey, England. In custom with the times for a daughter of nobility, Ada was "pawned" at age 16, but was rescued to marry her true love, Prince Henry of Scotland. Adventures and dangers of their medieval marriage are shared in *Pawn for a King*, published in 2019. A 3rd book in the "Pawn Series" of Ada's life and accomplishments is planned, along with a film series.

Made in the USA
Columbia, SC
20 December 2024

50238046R00111